Destiny's Drum

SELECTED FICTION WORKS BY L. RON HUBBARD

FANTASY
The Case of the Friendly Corpse

Death's Deputy

Fear

The Ghoul

The Indigestible Triton

Slaves of Sleep & The Masters of Sleep

Typewriter in the Sky

The Ultimate Adventure

SCIENCE FICTION
Battlefield Earth

The Conquest of Space

The End Is Not Yet

Final Blackout

The Kilkenny Cats

The Kingslayer

The Mission Earth Dekalogy*

Ole Doc Methuselah

To the Stars

ADVENTURE
The Hell Job series

WESTERN
Buckskin Brigades

Empty Saddles

Guns of Mark Jardine

Hot Lead Payoff

A full list of L. Ron Hubbard's
novellas and short stories is provided at the back.

*Dekalogy—a group of ten volumes

L. RON HUBBARD

Destiny's Drum

GALAXY
PRESS

Published by
Galaxy Press, LLC
7051 Hollywood Boulevard, Suite 200
Hollywood, CA 90028

Printed in the United States of America.

ISBN-10 1-59212-321-X
ISBN-13 978-1-59212-321-6

Library of Congress Control Number: 2007928445

Contents

Stories from Pulp Fiction's Golden Age

A ND it *was* a golden age.

The 1930s and 1940s were a vibrant, seminal time for a gigantic audience of eager readers, probably the largest per capita audience of readers in American history. The magazine racks were chock-full of publications with ragged trims, garish cover art, cheap brown pulp paper, low cover prices—and the most excitement you could hold in your hands.

"Pulp" magazines, named for their rough-cut, pulpwood paper, were a vehicle for more amazing tales than Scheherazade could have told in a million and one nights. Set apart from higher-class "slick" magazines, printed on fancy glossy paper with quality artwork and superior production values, the pulps were for the "rest of us," adventure story after adventure story for people who liked to *read*. Pulp fiction authors were no-holds-barred entertainers—real storytellers. They were more interested in a thrilling plot twist, a horrific villain or a white-knuckle adventure than they were in lavish prose or convoluted metaphors.

The sheer volume of tales released during this wondrous golden age remains unmatched in any other period of literary history—hundreds of thousands of published stories in over nine hundred different magazines. Some titles lasted only an issue or two; many magazines succumbed to paper shortages during World War II, while others endured for decades yet. Pulp fiction remains as a treasure trove of stories you can read, stories you can love, stories you can remember. The stories were driven by plot and character, with grand heroes, terrible villains, beautiful damsels (often in distress), diabolical plots, amazing places, breathless romances. The readers wanted to be taken beyond the mundane, to live adventures far removed from their ordinary lives—and the pulps rarely failed to deliver.

In that regard, pulp fiction stands in the tradition of all memorable literature. For as history has shown, good stories are much more than fancy prose. William Shakespeare, Charles Dickens, Jules Verne, Alexandre Dumas—many of the greatest literary figures wrote their fiction for the readers, not simply literary colleagues and academic admirers. And writers for pulp magazines were no exception. These publications reached an audience that dwarfed the circulations of today's short story magazines. Issues of the pulps were scooped up and read by over thirty million avid readers each month.

Because pulp fiction writers were often paid no more than a cent a word, they had to become prolific or starve. They also had to write aggressively. As Richard Kyle, publisher and editor of *Argosy,* the first and most long-lived of the pulps, so pointedly explained: "The pulp magazine writers, the best of them, worked for markets that did not write for critics or attempt to satisfy timid advertisers. Not having to answer to anyone other than their readers, they wrote about human beings on the edges of the unknown, in those new lands the future would explore. They wrote for what we would become, not for what we had already been."

Some of the more lasting names that graced the pulps include H. P. Lovecraft, Edgar Rice Burroughs, Robert E. Howard, Max Brand, Louis L'Amour, Elmore Leonard, Dashiell Hammett, Raymond Chandler, Erle Stanley Gardner, John D. MacDonald, Ray Bradbury, Isaac Asimov, Robert Heinlein—and, of course, L. Ron Hubbard.

In a word, he was among the most prolific and popular writers of the era. He was also the most enduring—hence this series—and certainly among the most legendary. It all began only months after he first tried his hand at fiction, with L. Ron Hubbard tales appearing in *Thrilling Adventures, Argosy, Five-Novels Monthly, Detective Fiction Weekly, Top-Notch, Texas Ranger, War Birds, Western Stories,* even *Romantic Range.* He could write on any subject, in any genre, from jungle explorers to deep-sea divers, from G-men and gangsters, cowboys and flying aces to mountain climbers, hard-boiled detectives and spies. But he really began to shine when he turned his talent to science fiction and fantasy of which he authored nearly fifty novels or novelettes to forever change the shape of those genres.

Following in the tradition of such famed authors as Herman Melville, Mark Twain, Jack London and Ernest Hemingway, Ron Hubbard actually lived adventures that his own characters would have admired—as an ethnologist among primitive tribes, as prospector and engineer in hostile climes, as a captain of vessels on four oceans. He even wrote a series of articles for *Argosy*, called "Hell Job," in which he lived and told of the most dangerous professions a man could put his hand to.

Finally, and just for good measure, he was also an accomplished photographer, artist, filmmaker, musician and educator. But he was first and foremost a *writer*, and that's the L. Ron Hubbard we come to know through the pages of this volume.

This library of Stories from the Golden Age presents the best of L. Ron Hubbard's fiction from the heyday of storytelling, the Golden Age of the pulp magazines. In these eighty volumes, readers are treated to a full banquet of 153 stories, a kaleidoscope of tales representing every imaginable genre: science fiction, fantasy, western, mystery, thriller, horror, even romance—action of all kinds and in all places.

Because the pulps themselves were printed on such inexpensive paper with high acid content, issues were not meant to endure. As the years go by, the original issues of every pulp from *Argosy* through *Zeppelin Stories* continue crumbling into brittle, brown dust. This library preserves the L. Ron Hubbard tales from that era, presented with a distinctive look that brings back the nostalgic flavor of those times.

L. Ron Hubbard's Stories from the Golden Age has something for every taste, every reader. These tales will return you to a time when fiction was good clean entertainment and the most fun a kid could have on a rainy afternoon or the best thing an adult could enjoy after a long day at work.

Pick up a volume, and remember what reading is supposed to be all about. Remember curling up with a *great story.*

—Kevin J. Anderson

KEVIN J. ANDERSON *is the author of more than ninety critically acclaimed works of speculative fiction, including The Saga of Seven Suns, the continuation of the Dune Chronicles with Brian Herbert, and his* New York Times *bestselling novelization of L. Ron Hubbard's* Ai! Pedrito!

Destiny's Drum

CHAPTER ONE

To Face a Firing Squad?

JOSÉ EMANUEL BATISTA'S voice flowed on like a river of crude oil—conversational, ingratiating in spite of the portent of his words.

"And then, *senhor*," said *Governador* Batista, "what may I be expected to do? You come here, attack my poor soldiers, laugh at them, and then refuse to state the reason you come to Kamling. What am I to believe?"

The white man, who lounged in the battered wicker chair on the other side of the more battered pine desk, returned no answer. His eyes were fastened on something outside the thatched hut.

The *governador* leaned forward. "And if, *senhor*, you are an international spy, come to survey the fortifications, I find it necessary to shoot you without delay. And if you are the only other thing you can be, an outlaw, also must I shoot you. In fact, *senhor*, I think it is best that I order out my firing squad immediately."

The white man sat up a little in his chair, still staring out the door. "What," he said, "is the name of that white girl out there?"

The *governador*'s smoothness fell away from him. An exasperated light entered his black, beady eyes. His several chins lopped over the edge of his white jacket collar and quivered there. It appeared that he had been struck a mortal blow.

The girl in question had swung down from her horse and had entered the trading post. Dust swirled in small geysers where her riding boots had left their imprint.

The white man turned, then, to give the *governador* more particular attention. "Now what was that you were talking about?"

The *governador*'s bushy brows were drawn down tight and his spiked mustache stood straight out from the round swarthy ball which was his face.

"*Senhor,*" he said, "you are insulting to my dignity of office."

"What office?"

"What office? *¡Por Dios!* Have you no respect whatever? The office of *governador* of the island of Kamling, jewel of the Banda Sea."

"Oh." A pack of black cigarettes lay on the *governador*'s desk. Taking one, the white man looked innocently into the official's face. "Have you a match?"

José Emanuel Batista sighed as quietly as possible and passed a paper package to the white man, a rugged young man in tattered white sailor pants. The young man's eyes were infinitely blue, infinitely languid. He was plainly bored.

"Let me go over this again, *senhor.* It is plain that you do not understand what you face. A firing squad!" The *governador* waved a dramatic hand across the street to a white wall.

"Is that all? *Governador,* it is much too warm to argue. If I am an international spy, shoot me. And if I am an outlaw, shoot me. But, for heaven's sake, don't talk so much!" He dragged upon the cigarette and braced his feet against the door jamb. The flimsy hut rocked perilously.

Once more the *governador* sighed. He glanced up at the face of the native who stood beside him. That face was brown, mostly filed teeth and lusterless eyes. The chin was resting on a naked wrist and the hand was holding a long, sharp spear. This was Aboo-Tabak, King of Kamling, though his regal robes consisted of a breechcloth and his badge of office was nothing more than a luminous-dialed, loudly ticking alarm clock which dangled about his scrawny throat.

"Aboo-Tabak," said the *governador*, "this man has insulted your office, my office, and the authority invested in us. What shall we do with him?"

"Eat him."

The white man laughed and took another drag from the black cigarette. "The government of Portugal forgot about this island thirty years ago and they've probably forgotten all about you as well."

"Continue!" ordered the *governador*.

"All right. I'll add that you're former Sergeant Duarte of the island of Timor, wanted for murder and a few other things. And that you blackbirded along here for a while known as Portuguese Joe."

"How do you know these things?"

The white man yawned and readjusted his feet. He kept a weather eye on the door of the trading post.

"I know them, that's all," he said. "Otherwise you wouldn't care whether I landed here or not, and you wouldn't put

5

yourself to such great pains to shoot me. Although you haven't asked it yet, my name is Sheridan."

The *governador*'s eyes glittered with amazement. "Sheridan!" he croaked. "Sheridan of the Nineteenth Route Army? That Sheridan?"

"I blush to admit it."

José Emanuel Batista sat back, rubbing his moist, fat palms together. "Then there is a chance that some of your rich friends might wish to buy you back again!"

"Not a chance. Go ahead and shoot me if you want. I'm tired of this."

"But wait," said the *governador*. "There is something you might do which would purchase your liberty."

"What?"

"Up above the town, three or four miles back from the edge of the sea, *senhor*, there is a man that causes me trouble."

"And," supplied Sheridan, "you want me to kill him for you."

"That's right."

"And what's he got that you want?"

"Oh, nothing, nothing, *senhor*. Has he, Aboo-Tabak?"

The King of Kamling shifted his weight on the spear. "Girl, gold. Sure, you want lots along that feller."

José Emanuel Batista smiled a sick smile. "He's lying, Sheridan. He gets those ideas now and then. The sun, you see."

Sheridan snorted. "Having heard a few stories about this Portuguese Joe, I'd rather believe a cannibal."

"Cannibal!" barked Aboo-Tabak, leaning forward on the spear. "I be Muslim, praise Allah!"

Sheridan grinned, though the dead viciousness in

Aboo-Tabak's eyes hardly invited such an expression. "But," said Sheridan, "if you're a follower of Allah, then why do you let yourself be ruled by an infidel dog of a Christian?"

"That's enough of that!" roared the *governador*, jumping to his feet.

Aboo-Tabak's eyes lingered on Portuguese Joe's fat shoulders which threatened to burst through the white duck jacket.

"Well, why?" insisted Sheridan.

Aboo-Tabak smiled, displaying yellow, pointed teeth. "He say someday he take me to town called . . . called . . ."

"Paris," supplied José Emanuel Batista, sitting down again. "Now, *senhor*, to return to our business again. As long as you refuse to kill this man for me, I see no other course but to let my regiment execute you. After all, *senhor*, you came here this morning, landed and immediately quarreled with my men."

"They tried to take my money and guns from me."

"That is a severe charge against my troops, *senhor*. You infer that they are bandits, eh?"

"Certainly," agreed Sheridan cheerfully. "But hold this up a moment, will you? The girl is coming out of the trading post."

The *governador* jumped up, almost upsetting his desk. He started out the door, but Sheridan's raised feet blocked him. With a grin Sheridan lowered the offending legs and stood upon them. He was almost a foot and a half taller than Portuguese Joe.

Across the street two soldiers rose up from their place at the base of the wall. They cradled their rifles across their arms and watched Sheridan with sleepy eyes.

The girl had mounted the small pony, after tying a bag of

supplies behind the saddle. She cantered toward the group which stood in the sun waiting for her. At first it appeared that she would pass by without a glance. Then she caught sight of Sheridan and pulled up.

The *governador* was at her side instantly, sweeping off his pith helmet in a grand bow. But the girl paid him no attention whatever. She was scowling at Sheridan. And Sheridan took note that she was beautiful even when she scowled. Her face was untouched by the violent sun and her blue gray eyes were steady and clear. She carried a Luger automatic holstered at her side.

"What are you doing here?" she demanded of Sheridan.

"I've been wondering myself."

"What's your name?"

"Sheridan."

Her eyes widened a little. "But what are you doing in this place?"

"I came down for my health. It was too rainy in China."

"Then you've come to the wrong address. It rains eight times a day here right now—and this is the dry season. What's this fat fool trying to do to you?"

"I beg the lady's pardon," wheezed Portuguese Joe. "Is it fitting that—"

"Don't believe anything he says."

"Well, I'm glad of that," Sheridan smiled. "He tells me he is about to set me up before a firing squad."

She whirled on the *governador*. "What's the meaning of this?"

"Now, now!" said José Emanuel Batista. "I was merely

having a little fun with Sheridan." He reached up and caught at her hand on the pommel.

Jerking her fingers away, the girl lifted her riding crop and brought it slashing down at José's cheek. Unfortunately, Aboo-Tabak had come closer to the horse and part of the blow struck his hands. Blood spurted from the cut on the *governador*'s face.

The horse shied at the sudden lunge of the two men. Aboo-Tabak's spear slashed up wickedly. José's fat hands fought to catch the girl's shoulders.

Abruptly both of them sprawled face down in the dust. Sheridan withdrew his foot and stood back. With a half bow he said, "Perhaps you'd better be on your way. There'll be a shooting here in little or no time."

The girl started to draw the Luger, but the two soldiers were already laying hold of Sheridan. José and Aboo-Tabak were jumping up, sending the dust feet high in their wrath.

Eyes wide, knowing that it was no use, the girl spurred forward. In a moment her horse was lost in the overhanging edge of the jungle, which lay over the hill before them.

"Now," said José, "we shall see whether or not I was fooling about that firing squad."

Aboo-Tabak stood with folded arms and his smile displayed his pointed teeth.

"Praise Allah," remarked Aboo-Tabak.

CHAPTER TWO

Wit Against Firearms

THE soldiers were barefooted, clad in ragged, faded denim from which the red piping had long since disappeared. They were Portuguese and their faces were almost as dark as the originals of this island of Kamling.

Sheridan—onetime Captain Phil Sheridan of this army and that—stood by and watched the "regiment" form its ranks. White dust rose up under the shuffling bare feet, adding another coat to apparently whitewashed toes. Sheridan's face was thoughtful, though his blue eyes were still languid. Among these people his six-foot stature gave him the appearance of Gulliver in Lilliput. The sun was blazing hot against the back of his torn white shirt.

From where he stood he could see the lagoon and its mangroves, which stood out of the water like old men on crutches. He could also see his sloop, beached by the departing tide. Turning and raising his eyes a little, he could see the tips of the white crosses in the walled cemetery above them, halfway up the shaggy hill.

He was aware of someone tugging at his sleeve. Looking down, he beheld the oily face of a man, questionably white. Clad in nothing more than a singlet and carpet slippers, the newcomer depended upon rimless glasses and silken cord to give him dignity.

"So they're going to shoot you, be they?"

Sheridan nodded. "So they tell me."

"Well, it won't be the first one they've shot. My name's Witherspoon. Charles Wesley Witherspoon." He offered a flabby hand which felt like a cold fish. "It's always my principle," he said, stifling a hiccup, "to be on hand at these executions."

"Like them?"

"Oh, no! But I like to pick me up a little business now and then. Y'see, besides running the trading post here, I'm a regularly ordained minister of the gospel and the undertaker."

"Do tell!" said Sheridan. "And what faith, may I ask?"

"Well," said Witherspoon cautiously, "that all depends. But I can say a nice little piece over your grave for you and I'll only charge you a couple pounds to do it, too. Be ye Catholic, by any chance?"

"No," replied Sheridan.

"Well, I just wanted to say that I'd forgot the Catholic burial service. Most any will do, won't it?"

"Most any."

"Well, there's a nice little plot up there that I can let you have for a couple more pounds. And for another bob I'll see to it that your name is marked right plain on it, too. Of course, I always like to have my payment in advance. There usually aren't any relatives, y'see."

Sheridan's eyes lit up. "So it's Holy Ben himself, is it?"

The rimless glasses slid off the nose. "How'd you know that?"

"Last time I saw you, you were shaking up drinks in Sloppy Ed's in Singapore."

"Did you now? But," he glanced swiftly around him, "don't let on about that."

"They never caught up to you, then?"

"You mean about that last killing?"

"But I guess you're safe enough here," said Sheridan. "This is the last spot they'd look for anybody. Right?"

"Yeah," said Holy Ben. "It got too hot for me down in the Java Sea."

"Well, then, Reverend Witherspoon, if they get me this time, bury away."

"Funny," said Holy Ben, "how everybody knows everybody else in these parts. Now I know'd ye when I first set eyes on ye. You're Capt'n Sheridan, isn't it?"

"This, my dear reverend, is a pretty small part of a small world."

José Emanuel Batista waddled up, still glowering. His sword spanked him as he walked. "We are ready, *senhor*. Are there any last requests?"

"You mean," said Sheridan, "that you think that ragtag, bobtail bunch of nitwits can shoot straight enough to kill a man?"

"Are you insulting my regiment?"

"Sure. I'll lay you a bet of ten dollars that they don't even know left from east."

José made a sign to the two soldiers behind Sheridan. They came out of their lethargy and boosted him up against the white wall. Before Sheridan twenty men were leaning on their rifles, sweating in the heat. José whipped a much-used black cloth out of his white jacket.

13

Sheridan turned and observed the wall behind him. Its cracked surface was dotted with bullet holes. He eyed José. "I'll still bet those monkeys can't hit me the first volley."

José quivered and began to affix the black cloth. Then his arms relaxed a little. "How much do you bet?"

"A thousand dollars that they don't even know the manual of arms!"

"And how do I know you have a thousand dollars?"

Sheridan smiled. "You took a checkbook away from me this morning. I'll sign a check on the Bank of Shanghai and give it to the Reverend Witherspoon to hold. I'll give them some orders in their own language, and if they obey them you win. Otherwise, I tear up my check, and you can donate yours to charity."

"I always heard, *senhor,* that you were crazy. Now I know it. However, I lose nothing by accepting your money. You die anyway." José Emanuel Batista stepped back, pocketing the black cloth for the moment. An orderly brought the checkbook and an indelible pencil and Sheridan wrote on his knee.

Straightening, Sheridan smiled again. "All right. Now I'll give them a few simple orders, and if they obey, you win."

"You mean, I win anyway. But proceed. I wish to show that you lie."

Standing where he was, against the wall, Sheridan barked, "*¡Orden armas!* Order arms!"

The line listlessly let their rifle butts thud in the dust. Sheridan shook his head at the *governador,* pityingly. José's lips tightened as though his entire dignity was at stake.

"Right shoulder arms!" cried Sheridan. The movement

was executed with a sloppy weariness. José harangued them from the sidelines.

"Port arms!" barked Sheridan. "Right shoulder arms! Port arms! Right-face! Left-face!"

More words from José caused the Portuguese to fumble nervously at their rifles.

"They are not doing it right!" Sheridan jeered.

"Better than yourself!" snapped José.

Sheridan stepped to his guard and took the rifle from his hands. "Here. Watch this." And with movements as fast as light the rifle went through the Princess Pat manual—a dizzy, spinning sight of sun on polished steel. The eyes of the soldiers widened. Sheridan handled a nine-pound gun as though it were a walking stick.

Leaning on the rifle, Sheridan said, "Now let's see you do that. Order arms! Right shoulder arms! Order arms! At trail, left-face. Right-face! About-face!"

Dazed by the swift orders, the soldiers spun about on bare heels. A long wailing cry came from the *governador*, for, on the instant of execution, Sheridan slung the rifle over his back and vaulted the wall. He sprinted toward the cemetery, and before any semblance of order came from below, he had leaped over the second wall and was running between the mounds and leaning crosses to the inviting jungle on the other side.

José, left far below, immediately ordered a volley. It rattled through the palm trees over Sheridan's head. Another volley followed before the first had lost its echo, but by that time Sheridan had struck the path which led to the top of the cliff and was almost lost to sight.

At the top Sheridan stopped and threw himself behind a felled palm trunk. He was out of breath after his long uphill run and the sweat was pouring down his face. He tugged at the brim of his cap and then adjusted the rifle sights.

The soldiers were already swarming over the cemetery wall, knocking the crosses in every direction. A fact not so gruesome as it might sound, for the rains had long ago washed the faces of the wood of any and every name.

José Emanuel Batista toiled in the rear of his "regiment," swearing and sweating mightily. Aboo-Tabak still stood outside the government hut, considering such a chase far beneath his dignity. Besides, it was too hot. Charles Wesley Witherspoon stood in rapt study of the check Sheridan had written, wondering, doubtless, the best way to alter the payee's name.

Sheridan took a bead on José's pith helmet. The rifle leaped in his hands and the helmet rolled back down the hill. Startled, José stopped and then proceeded to flop down behind the near wall of the burying ground.

"Come on, you buckos!" bawled Sheridan. "Do you want to live forever?"

Evidently most of the soldiers had that thought in mind and were very desirous of achieving such a feat. They scuttled like hound-harassed rabbits into the undergrowth. Sheridan crouched down behind the slick-barked tree and watched. He knew that they would try to flank him and that he was not yet free to run.

José was screaming at his men from the protection of the wall. He used every known curse and reviled every known

ancestor of each man, but still no soldiers were brash enough
to venture out of hiding.

In the spot he had chosen, Sheridan was glad of the shade
and the cool wind which was coming in from the silken blue
sea. He estimated that he could skirt the group and make his
sloop if he tried, but he decided that the time for running
had not yet arrived. There were other things to be done here.

After an hour the mosquitoes found him and circled his
head as Indians circled oxcarts on the western plains. Their
monotonous drone was lulling and, as to their bites, Sheridan
was too inured to them to mind.

Aboo-Tabak had seated himself against José's hut. Time
was nothing to him, in spite of the alarm clock which dangled
about his throat. Three of Aboo-Tabak's headmen came to
him and seated themselves by his side. All four pairs of eyes
rested listlessly on the crest of the hill, patiently waiting.

Sheridan knew that the time of sacrifice to *Duadillah* was
near at hand and Mohammedanism was not securely enough
entrenched to cause these people to forgo so ancient a custom.
The sun god was much more interesting than Allah at such
times, because the Koran, remarkably enough, does not make
any mention of the legality of cannibalism.

Timor, a great, far-reaching blur on the horizon, was easily
seen from the crest of the island. But Timor, with its Dutch
law and order, paid as little attention to Kamling as a man
pays an ant. Kamling was one of sixty-six islands, forgotten
because, down below the line, it's much too warm to worry
about empire.

And from the crest Sheridan could see something else. A

field of rice was being attended by men who were suspiciously close together. A chain gang, obviously, enslaved from the upper reaches, perhaps, for the purpose of enriching José Emanuel Batista. No wonder, thought Sheridan, that José was so insistent about shooting casual visitors. Or had José known that his visit was far from casual? One thing was certain. If you shoot a man dead, he is unlikely to carry stories back to civilization.

A shrub moved to the right, moved against the breeze. Sheridan's muscles tightened. A face was indistinct through the leaves. Sheridan made no sound. The face came near and the leaves moved with greater violence. Down the hill José's ranting voice went on, monotony itself.

One of the Portuguese soldiers jumped erect in front of Sheridan. The man was not relying upon a mere rifle; he had a two-foot bolo held aloft, ready for the downswing. The keen edge sang through the air. Sheridan's head was against the trunk, directly in the blade's path. His rifle leaped to one side and spat flame. The blade buried itself in the palm and stayed there. The soldier toppled backward, clawing at nothing. The bullet had jackknifed him. He rolled for minutes before he brought up against the cemetery wall close to José.

When the dust cleared, Sheridan jacked another bullet into the chamber and lay down once more. Close by he saw another bush shake. He sent a slug through the underbrush. A blue denim figure rolled out.

Shrill screams rose in panic all down the slope. Bare feet trampled through the foliage. Rifles were disregarded in the rush to get down and out of sight before another random shot should snuff out another life.

Sheridan opened the breech and blew the smoke out of it before he put another cartridge in place. He waited for some minutes before he was satisfied that no others were near him.

Inching back out of sight, he stood up and draped the gun over his arm. A voice behind him was cool and slow.

"Good shooting, white."

Sheridan turned slowly. At first he saw nothing but a silver-mounted pistol, double-barreled, in a brown hand. Then his eyes came up to the level of a shark-teeth necklace and at last rested on a brown, smooth face. This was a native, but no ordinary Polynesian. The shark-teeth necklace was the badge of chief.

The man was almost as tall as Sheridan and as well built. He leaned languidly against a tree trunk, holding the heavy, ancient pistol with no effort whatever.

"Thanks," said Sheridan.

"Go back and shoot some more," ordered the native.

"Nobody else to shoot."

"Nobody in town even though?"

"Rifle won't carry that far."

"Well, shoot anyway." The native raised the pistol ever so slightly.

"What's the matter?" smiled Sheridan. "Don't you like that gang down there?" His ears picked up the sound of feet coming up the path. They evidently knew that he had left his stand at the crest.

"No," said the native. "No like them feller."

19

"They're coming up the path now," said Sheridan. "Can't we postpone this parley a little while? How about making a date with you tomorrow morning?"

"You afraid them feller?"

"Who, me? Well, there are quite a few of them."

"Listen. Them come close right away even though. You shoot a one or maybe two, three, huh?"

"I'm afraid it's too late. They'd nail us as soon as we showed our heads now." Sheridan, disregarding the pistol, started off down the path toward the deeper jungle. The pistol prodded him.

"You not go no place," said the native. "You got rifle. We fight with them. Me, I'm King Kobo. King of Kamling even though."

"How about Aboo-Tabak?" Sheridan glanced over his shoulder. There was no cover here and in a moment he was certain that José's men would try to top the crest.

"Aboo-Tabak Mohammedan. Me Christian, except today. Today first day of feast to *Duadillah*. Me, I come down here to get one fine man for feast even though."

"Can't we postpone this? Talk later? How about it?"

A blue cap came over the edge, only to bob back again as soon as Sheridan came into sight. Sheridan dropped on one knee and leveled the rifle. A second blue cap bobbed up and disappeared too rapidly for a shot.

"Lot of them, huh?" said King Kobo, still leaning against his tree. "Maybe it be better not to fight this day even though. Me, I think I better go over to my town now."

Lowering the gun, the native walked away, very erect.

Sheridan sped in the opposite direction. When he had reached the edge of the heavy undergrowth he stopped. A soldier was crawling behind the fallen palm. Sheridan contented himself with sending the man's cap flying through the air. Then he turned and sprinted as fast as the ripping thorn bushes would allow. In a few minutes he entered into another trail which ran parallel with the first.

Trotting down this, he saw that he was nearing an open space ahead. He thought for a moment that he would circle this and he would have, had not an automatic barked in front of him. The slug ripped through the branches over his head.

He stopped and lowered the rifle to the ground. He could see the outline of a pith helmet in the dimness before him, also a ray of sunlight dancing off a gun.

"Now what?" said Sheridan with a sigh.

CHAPTER THREE

Sorry Kilton—Wanted in Shanghai

L IGHT rays fell across the path in kaleidoscopic patterns, moving, ever changing, as the wind in the treetops swung the fronds. Three parrots came to rest on a swaying bough and chattered briefly before they fell to watching the tableau underneath their cloudless highway.

It was twilight down among the ferns and brush, but it was deadly hot with an oppressive heat which seemed to clog the air until it was unfit to breathe.

Sheridan's brow was damp. A globule of sweat ran down into his left eye and stung him, but he did not move. He watched the almost motionless gun barrel which protruded through the greenness. After a bit, he knew, the wielder of the gun would recover enough to show himself—and until that nerve was sufficiently recovered, Sheridan wanted no words to pass.

At last the pipe-clayed helmet moved. A slim white hand parted the branches and the girl of his former acquaintance appeared. Her face was partially masked in shadow, but her lips were tight.

"Why have you come here?" she demanded in a cool voice.

"Because it seemed like a good idea."

"You're lying."

"Far be it from me to question a lady's word, ma'am."

"Didn't they tell you that men died when they approached this point on the island?"

Sheridan smiled slightly. "They only informed me that I was about to be shot. If I'm committing any breach of etiquette, may I beg your pardon?"

"Then . . . well, if you didn't know, I suppose it's all right for me to let you go back."

"Certainly. I'd gladly be shot if it would do a lady any good."

"Shot! Oh . . . I thought that was just a show they were putting on for my benefit. Or I thought they were trying to force some information out of you."

"No, they were going to shoot all right—live bullets and everything."

"Then . . . then you can't go back down that way!"

"No. I can't, begging your pardon."

"And you can't stay here or go any further inland. What are you going to do?"

"If I had led an exemplary life, I'd die and go to heaven."

She lowered the Luger until it pointed at the strip of ground between them. Her eyes, two light-gray jewels set in shadow, studied Sheridan.

He started toward her, but she raised the gun again.

"You haven't anything to fear from me," he said.

"How do I know that?"

"You must have something pretty valuable hidden in these jungles, to be so insistent about it. What is it? Can't be emeralds. And you couldn't hide a rubber plantation."

"There's no use guessing, Mr. Sheridan. You'll never find out."

"Well, there's only one thing which puzzles me. And that's why old man Kilton is so exclusive these days."

"Old man Kilton!"

"Sure. Sorry Kilton, late of the China Coast. You should have heard of him, seeing that he's your dad."

Her eyes bored into him and through him. Forgotten, the Luger sank down. "You know Sorry Kilton?"

"Why shouldn't I? He and I are just like that." Sheridan raised two fingers. "But I didn't know he had a daughter."

"In a moment," said the girl evenly, "you'll know a little too much."

"I know too much already. If you told Sorry Kilton that you sent Phil Sheridan back to the wolves, he'd take a stick to you. If you won't believe it, take me down the trail to your compound and Sorry Kilton will prove it for me."

Doubtfully, the girl looked back along the trail. "But he said not to bring *anyone*," she muttered.

"How did he know that Phil Sheridan would come along?"

"I . . . I guess you're right. Come along."

Grinning, Sheridan threw the rifle sling over his shoulders and followed her into the thicket where she had staked her horse. He held the reins until she mounted and then passed them up to her. She still held the Luger.

"That's a nice gun," commented Sheridan. "Sorry was always one to collect good side arms." With a quick jerk of his wrist, Sheridan reached up and seized the gun. She tried to cling to it, but it was twisted toward her thumb and she could not.

Thrusting the weapon into his belt, Sheridan smiled up at her. "It will be much safer here, in case we're jumped by José's boys. I guess they'll be combing the woods for me."

She glared at him and tried to spur away, but he caught the side of the bit and held the pony in. Quickly he struck out down the trail, as though nothing had happened. They went on for some minutes in silence. Then Sheridan glanced back at her.

"Do you know this fellow Kobo? King Kobo?"

"He's a murdering, cutthroat cannibal. What about him?"

"Met him a while ago. He thought I was a pretty good shot."

"He'd think anyone was a good shot who killed someone for him. I suppose he tried to get you to kill Aboo-Tabak."

"No, but he looked hopeful. Tell me some more."

The girl shook her head and remained silent until they had passed a deep bend in the uphill trail. "What are you doing here?" she asked bluntly.

"I sometimes wonder myself. What's your name, Miss Kilton?"

"Patsy. And it's *Miss* Kilton to you. If you aren't a friend of Sorry's, there'll be trouble brewing by the bucketful, Mr. Sheridan."

"You think he'll kill me, that it?"

"Certainly he will. He's the fastest draw and best shot from Australia to Taku."

"Except another fellow I knew."

"Your conceit is distasteful."

"I cannot tell a lie, Patsy. That's my only fault."

"Hmph! We'll see what we shall see. I think you're a spy."

"You do! Spies wear green whiskers and pink spectacles. And I, dear Patsy, am an honorable man. Is that your clearing just ahead?"

Patsy Kilton gave no answer, but from the expression on her face her reply would obviously have been in the affirmative. They walked near to the edge of the trees and Sheridan was about to step out into the clear sunshine when Patsy cried out in a small voice.

"Don't go nearer!" she pleaded. "Listen to me, Mr. Sheridan. Don't go up to the house. Sorry might be there, and if you aren't a friend of his he might—"

"Never fear," said Sheridan and strode onward. He dropped the reins and one palm lingered near the butt of the Luger automatic. He rocked forward like a stalking panther. The girl watched him with wide, fearful eyes.

Halfway across the compound there was a movement in the door of the thatched hut. A tall, gangling man stepped out and started to wave to Patsy. Midway through the gesture he caught sight of Sheridan, who was slightly to the right.

The gangling one's hands blurred. Flame spat from Sheridan's waist. A slug imbedded itself not an inch from the gangling man's ear.

"Hello, Kilton," said Sheridan evenly.

Kilton's hands fell slack before the muzzle of the Luger. Then they began a slow, balky ascent until they were elevated over his head.

"What do you want this time, Sheridan?" whispered Kilton.

"Something to eat, a place to sleep. That's all. I'm not out for blood, Kilton, and I'm willing to forget about the past if you are."

"I'm not likely to forget, Sheridan."

"Then I'll have to put a bullet in you where you stand."

Kilton drew nearer, hands still up. He was tall, taller even than Sheridan. His face was long and sad as the face of a bloodhound. His mustaches drooped, stained brown at the ends from constant contact with tobacco. Kilton was dressed in a blue serge suit which had last been pressed in Shanghai some time back. The coat sagged and its pockets bulged. His belt drooped. His pants were thrust into a run-over pair of mining boots. But in direct contrast to his outward appearance, Kilton's eyes were light and keen. And in further contrast, the two revolvers which sagged at the hips were as brilliant as new silver.

"Why did you come down here, anyway?" he said.

"It's a long story, and you wouldn't be interested. I might ask you why you're here, but I don't have to, I know you too well. That shack of yours is built on a sidehill. The dirt in this compound is crushed rock. That rusty mass of junk over there was once a winch.

"Kilton, you're down here mining for gold and you're getting gold. The tunnel is under the house, and you're spreading your dump to keep our pal Portuguese Joe off the scent."

"Pretty clever, Sheridan."

"Isn't it, though? But you aren't fooling Portuguese Joe a bit and you aren't fooling me, so why go to all this trouble?"

"You know all the answers, Sheridan. Go ahead."

"I'm not out for blood, Kilton, and I'm willing to forget about the past if you are."

"Because you don't want anybody to get wind of this affair and throw this probably illegal concession to the breeze. A mining man like yourself knows what litigation means to a paying mine."

"Pretty clever."

"Sure, Kilton, but that isn't the real reason."

"No?"

"No. The bankers up in Shanghai, so I hear, have put a big price on your head. And they're anxious to pay out blood money—big money."

"And you're here to collect it!"

"Nuts!"

"Well, what else can a guy think?"

"I don't care what you think. You aren't the only one that's the subject of a wad of blood money."

"So you finally got in trouble!"

Sheridan nodded. "And I came down here so you'd have company."

"And if I don't want company?"

"Then you'll be all alone in the cold, cold ground, massa."

"You talk mighty pert on the end of a gun."

"I've heard you make a few comments while in that position. Isn't so funny to be on the outside looking in, is it? By the way, that's a pretty girl you've got, Kilton."

"I'd advise you not to look at her."

"Don't worry—I'm not like the rest of your pals. I'm just thinking about Portuguese Joe. He tried something this afternoon."

Patsy came abreast of her father.

Kilton stared at her. "You mean that greasy so-and-so got funny with you?"

"Yes, Dad."

"What happened?"

"Mr. Sheridan tripped him." The remembrance of it made her eyes light up. "And Portuguese Joe hit the dirt face down and got that nice white uniform all covered with dust, and Aboo-Tabak was spitting dirt and Polynesian by the yard."

"And then what happened?"

"Why . . . why, they fell down, that's all, and I rode away."

"And left Sheridan right there with them?"

"Well, I couldn't—"

"Don't tell me what you couldn't do!" stormed Kilton. "You had a gun, didn't you?"

"Well, yes, but—"

"And Sheridan didn't have one, did he?"

"No, but you see—"

"Do I see what? I ought to lick you! Haven't I brought you up better than that? Haven't I? There are enough coldblooded devils in this part of the world without my daughter turning into one. You had a gun and Portuguese Joe was in the dust, and you didn't make any attempt to get this man out of it?"

"No, I rode toward the—"

Sorry Kilton turned to Sheridan, forgetting all about the gun. "I'm plumb sorry, Sheridan," he said, holding out his hand. "I thought I raised this girl of mine to be a better gentleman than that. Let me apologize for her."

Sheridan shoved the Luger into his waistband once more and shook Kilton's hand. "She couldn't do anything else. By the way, how did you know all about this?"

"I didn't. But I did know that you'd been in a scrap of some sort and that she hadn't. From the looks of your clothes, you see."

"Why, that's all right," Sheridan began.

"No, it isn't either. It plumb knocks the props out from under me to know that Patsy'd let anyone cover her retreat for her."

Patsy's eyes, when Sheridan glanced up at her, were on the ground.

"Oh, well," said Sorry Kilton, "maybe she'll learn someday. Come on inside, Sheridan, and have a drink. I'm sorry about this little unpleasantness."

They walked toward the door and were about to enter when the jungle burst apart under the onslaught of strident voices.

"Those are Aboo-Tabak's jackals," said Kilton, with narrow eyes. "I reckon we'd better postpone that drink until we load up that rack of rifles over there against the wall."

CHAPTER FOUR

Portuguese Joe Scents Gold

A scarlet lory came down from a fig tree like a streak of blood, notes of alarm tumbling from its red throat. A water buffalo lumbered across the compound snorting, horns lowered, his piggish eyes gleaming.

Sheridan buckled a brace of automatics about his waist, smiling at Patsy. She spent several seconds watching his deft hands before she turned to the stack of wooden boxes which held rifle ammunition.

Sorry Kilton gave the clearing a doleful stare and leaned on a short Lee-Enfield rifle. "They'll be sending a flag of truce out here in a minute. I'd admire to plug that fat lout José."

"Maybe we'll get the chance," said Sheridan. "But I hate to let you folks in for all this. After all, he's on my trail, not yours."

"He's on ours too," countered Kilton. "There's a chest—Well, he'd like to rummage around here right smart if I'd let him."

"You were going to mention the gold," said Sheridan. "I heard Aboo-Tabak say something about that. And something about Patsy. Hope you've got that stuff well hidden."

"Sure I have. What do you take me for?"

"Well, this isn't the China Coast. Up there they know enough to leave you alone. Afraid of you in fact. But Portuguese Joe might be just dumb enough to let you plug him."

"I hope he's dumber than that," said Kilton.

"Hope you don't think I'm being too personal," said Sheridan, "but I would like to know what deal made you light out from China and land in this spot."

Kilton shifted his baleful eyes and then resumed his watch of the clearing edge. "You tell him, Patsy."

Patsy Kilton, her hands full of cartridge belts, looked up from where she sat on an empty packing case. A small smudge of Cosmoline was on her nose and her sun helmet was tipped far back, allowing her golden hair to cascade down over her eyes. She brushed the silky mist away and looked up at Sheridan.

"There isn't much to tell. Dad rode up to the school where he'd put me two years before and told me to get on the spare horse and ride the devil, and I did. Later on we located a sailing schooner, boarded it and landed down here. We landed after shooting a couple of these Portuguese soldiers and managed to get our equipment up here to this spot. Seems as if Dad located this place some years ago, while Portuguese Joe was too busy blackbirding to bother about make-believe government."

"That's good," said Sheridan. "But how did you get into trouble in Shanghai?"

"Tell him, Patsy. He probably knows anyhow."

Patsy, somewhat annoyed at this constant interruption

in her work of clipping bullets, threw back the hair again. "Dad let some of the Shanghai bankers in on a swell deal he had mapped out. Mining, you know—a gold vein in the Solomons. They put up heavy cash. Dad ran into some hard luck with the natives, and a charge of dynamite was set off in the wrong place and the vein was lost forever. So Dad went up to Shanghai to explain things to those fellows."

"And what happened?"

"They told him that when a bank went broke in Shanghai, it was customary to execute the bank president—which, I suppose, is very true, and probably a good law. And this two hundred thousand they'd given Dad was all that stood between them and a bank failure. So they built on Dad's reputation as a gunman, shot a couple of their own clerks, made it look like a robbery and pinned the whole thing on Dad. That let them out. Now, to save their face, I suppose they're offering a reward for Dad."

"Very logical." Sheridan walked to the door. "See anything yet?"

"No," Kilton replied. "That's the trouble. I don't see near enough. Watch that clump over there at the left. My boys are housed on the other side of that, and I haven't heard a word out of them."

"Maybe they sold out to the enemy."

"I guess so," Kilton said, wearily. "No, there's one of them now."

A brown-skinned fellow, almost six feet tall, sprinted through the underbrush toward them. As is the custom in the

Timor Laut, his hair was dyed with a sticky gilt substance. Panting, he came to a stop before Kilton, saluting with his hand against his sweaty forehead. His sarong, blue and red, was torn by the brush he had run through.

"Hy you, massa! Ringu gone away along village fella."

"Ringu!" growled Kilton. "You mean they took him!"

"Hy you! No, massa. Ringu like to go."

"Ringu's my foreman," said Kilton. "He's deserted to the enemy!"

"Good riddance," said Sheridan.

Kilton spat. "Good riddance, hell! I taught that boy all he knew, and I need him."

"Let him go," said Patsy from her packing case. "We've got enough."

Kilton glared at her. Then he drilled the native with the colored hair. "You! Bring up the rest of the boys!"

"No, sir. They not come."

"Hell! All right, I'll go down there and protect their measly necks for them. Sheridan, will you stay here with Patsy for a while? If I can, I'll bring my crew back up here."

Kilton bent over and started to run to the edge of the trees, followed by the brown native. But before the Tennessean's long frame entered the fringe of trees, a blue rifle barrel was thrust from beneath a shrub.

Sheridan saw the gun and acted in the same instant. An automatic came up and belched a ribbon of blue powder smoke. The wielder of the rifle fell out of the cover and twitched for an instant. His glazed eyes studied the sky, closed and then opened again. The arms flopped weakly. Sheridan waved at Kilton, who immediately disappeared.

Turning around, Sheridan saw Patsy's horrified eyes. "Sorry," he said. "I had to shoot kind of fast. If I'd thought, I'd have dropped him backward and out of sight."

Patsy's big, gray blue eyes fixed themselves on Sheridan's face. Realizing that he'd said the wrong thing, he squinted industriously through the sunlight, looking for further targets.

At the expiration of five minutes, a questionably white square of cloth was raised to flap over a small tree. Sheridan turned to Patsy.

"Yell at them to send their party over here. I guess they think Sorry is still with us."

Patsy had recovered herself, and although she avoided looking at the dead man who sprawled against the reddish ground, her voice was even.

"Come ahead!" she called.

A white shape bulked out of the undergrowth and edged toward the thatched hut. José Emanuel Batista was making very sure that the coast was clear. Simultaneous with his appearance leaves moved along the fringe of green, denoting the positions of posted scouts and snipers.

Patsy stood in the doorway, watching. Portuguese Joe halted halfway over and stood with his hand on his sword hilt, posing.

"Well, aren't you going to send your father out to me, Miss Kilton?"

"If you want to talk to anyone, come inside."

Portuguese Joe looked aggrieved. "That's contrary to all rules, Miss Kilton. The truce party should be met halfway."

"Wars are fought by gentlemen," Patsy retorted. "If I did right, I'd make you go around to the servant's entrance—if we had one."

Portuguese Joe reproved her with sorrowful eyes. Nevertheless he stepped forward, trying not to waddle, and mounted the steps. Head very erect, as though he owned all the ground he trod, he walked the width of the porch and entered the room. He stopped there, his mouth agape.

Sheridan was standing squarely before him, hands on the butts of his guns, cap set at a rakish angle. His eyes were harder and brighter than diamonds.

"Why—where is Mr. Kilton, *senhorita*?"

"He's away on a business trip." Sheridan's voice crackled. "Maybe while you're here, you'd like to hear a funny story?"

"But I thought—"

"I know what you thought. You thought Kilton would have me tied up in the corner, ready to hand over to you. And you thought that he would see to it that a flag of truce—so-called—would be respected. Well, Kilton isn't here, and I'm in charge of this shebang. Now I'll go on with my funny story."

"No. I'm sure that—"

"You want to hear this?"

"Why, yes, *senhor*. But my men—"

Sheridan smiled crisply. "Yes, your men. You have them posted out there along the edge. And as soon as Kilton showed himself they would have plugged him. That's the way you do business. Now about this funny story—"

"Really, *senhor,* I must—"

"While I was down in the Malay States, we had a war with a datto. He laid siege to our compound for three weeks—"

"Really, *senhor*—!"

"We were about out of water and food, so we sent a messenger out to this chief to tell him that he could come inside and hear our surrender, but that he had to come in person."

"*Senhor,* if—"

"And so this chief came inside the fence all dressed up fit to kill. We bowed him into a chair and he sat down. I remember how he looked right now. He was fat and greasy and brown. About your height, he was. And when he came he had about the same look on his face that you did."

"*Senhorita,* if your father—"

"So," continued Sheridan, blithely, "he sat down in the chair, and he was ready to hear our terms of surrender. Now we knew if we surrendered he'd have us executed immediately, and we didn't intend to have that happen. So we took cords—"

"My men, *senhor*—"

Sheridan drew a bolo out of his belt and hefted it, feeling of its keen edge. "So I took this very knife that I have here and walked up to the datto like this." Sheridan closed the distance until less than a foot intervened. "And then I took his hand and I cut off a finger. I remember the finger twitched. It had a ring on it, too.

"And so I threw this thing over the fence to the chief's troops. They knew what it was, but they didn't do anything, so I cut off another finger. And when I threw the second finger over the fence, the troops still didn't have anything to say."

"*Senhor* Sheridan—"

"Well, that was too slow for me, so I cut off his whole hand the next time and threw it over. That didn't work, so I went right on cutting. Boy, how he howled! Just as though it was hurting him!

"To shorten this funny story, after a while that datto was pretty close to dead. Looked just like you did, too. Fat stomach—wore a white jacket that was choking him all the time."

"Uh, *senhor,* I must—"

"Well, the funny part of the story is this. When he was about dead, the finger was tossed back over the wall at me, with a little note attached. The note said, 'Why don't you throw over his head?'"

Portuguese Joe was sweating through every pore. His white jacket had wilted. He stepped toward the door, not daring to take his eyes off Sheridan and the knife, aware of Patsy standing against the wall, gun in hand. Portuguese Joe managed to step over the sill before his nerve broke. He whirled like a top and ran, arms flying, helmet bobbing, on a mad dash back to the cover of the trees.

"That," said Sheridan coolly, "is the fastest run I've ever seen a man make. And that," he continued, "was the biggest whopper I ever told. I don't think this attack will continue very long."

Patsy laughed, her eyes dancing. She sank down on a packing case, still laughing. Sheridan went to the door.

From the woods came the sound of moving feet and the occasional clank of rifles and cartridge belts hitting together. Shortly, nothing moved in the trees but birds, and the silence of the hills settled down upon the clearing.

Twenty minutes later Kilton came back, running, arms flapping at his sides. At first Sheridan thought the man was mystified at the disappearance of the troops, but that illusion was rapidly dispelled. Kilton drew up panting.

"That fella Ringu," said Kilton.

"What about him?"

"Sold out all right." Kilton shrugged. "Now I've got to do it all over again."

"Do what all over?" said Sheridan.

"The mining. And the vein is almost gone. It was a vein of wire gold in the first place, and it's bound to pinch out, that wire gold. But maybe there's a little of it left."

"What's wrong, Dad?"

Kilton pinned Patsy with his glance. "Wrong! Plenty wrong! That fella Ringu knew where we cached the gold, and he told those others about it. It's been dug up, the chest and everything!"

Patsy turned away and stared at the thatched hut. "And I thought we were all through with living here!"

"That's easy," said Sheridan. "I'll run down to the village and get it back for you."

Kilton shook his head. "That can't be done by anybody, not even you. It's probably hid again someplace else. It's gone, and that's all there is to it. This frontal attack was just a coverup for the boys who were digging up the chest I buried the bullion in."

Sheridan walked to the fringe of the trees and gazed down a path. He turned and motioned to Kilton.

When the lanky Tennessean had come to his side, Sheridan pointed mutely down the path.

A brown man was there, pinned tight against a tree by three spears which had been driven though his body. A knife protruded from his mouth and through the back of his skull. Ants were already swarming over the corpse.

"Ringu!" said Kilton meaningly.

CHAPTER FIVE

If They Can Use Kobo

DINNER that night was unusual, because a big can of green peas, saved for company purposes, had been opened and heated. Besides this, there were no other Northern dishes. The yellow-white, pithy breadfruit which tasted like dry summer squash, fresh papayas and mangoes, and the bread made from native corn constituted the regular fare.

Patsy Kilton presided, dressed in clean white drill, the last of her once ample wardrobe. Kilton met the occasion by brushing some of the dust from his blue serge coat and by combing his mustache.

"Patsy here," said Kilton, dipping his corn bread in a saucer of molasses, "was brought up right. That's why I feel bad about this business of the missing chest. I thought I could take her back to Tennessee. I've got a big place back there—white pillars out in front, and a lawn big enough for three crops of corn. Got a lake, too. There are lots of nice young fellas around there who could take her to dances and such. Damn my hide, anyway; I shouldn't have trusted that Ringu!"

"Can't the place support itself?" said Sheridan, sipping the pannikin of scalding coffee.

"Support itself!" Kilton snorted. "You're talking through your sun hat, mister! That land in northeastern Tennessee is the best looking in the whole US—best coon hunting, best people—but don't you ever kid yourself that it'll grow anything but weeds!"

"I heard," said Sheridan, "that they were putting in a big nitrogen fertilizer plant down in Muscle Shoals. That is, they were going to start up the one they had there already. That ought to do the trick."

"Sheridan"—Kilton reached for more corn pone—"I'm a good mining engineer, but a hell of a farmer. Isn't that right, Patsy?"

Patsy smiled. "You're right when you say you're a good mining engineer, Dad. And you're right about farming. And if you wanted to admit it, you could say a whole lot about what you don't know in a business line."

"Say, young lady!"

"Now don't interrupt me!" Patsy held up her hand. "You had enough and more when you started that Solomon Island place. You sank your money into it, and now we haven't anything, and you've even lost your reputation. I wanted to leave this place last month, but you said there were two stringers you hadn't cleaned out—and now look what's happened! Oh, I'm not pulling you on the carpet, and I'm not kicking. I can stand a thatched hut just as long as you can."

"Now, I hate to hear you say that about business, Patsy," said Kilton. "I want to go home with a big stake, see? A *big* stake. And then—"

"Sorry Kilton," cried Patsy, "don't spring that on me again! I do believe that you don't want to go home. You like to fight too well!"

Kilton leaned back in his chair and laughed. "And you

don't think I'd get my fill of fighting back there in Tennessee? Honey, that's where all our famous fighters came from. No fighting man was any account unless he was born in Tennessee."

Sheridan laughed.

"Unless he was born—" Kilton gave Sheridan a blank stare. "Say, where *were* you born, anyway?"

Sheridan laughed, his teeth sparkling in the lantern light. "Virginia."

"Unless he comes from Virginia," Kilton finished soberly.

Patsy stared at the door as though listening.

"What's up, Patsy?" asked Sheridan.

"I heard the sound of a horn. And I thought I could hear the beat of a drum."

"Probably so," Kilton agreed. "Old King Kobo will go *Duadillah* for the next week, and then he'll be a Christian again."

"I met him today," Sheridan said.

"You met him and walked away alive?"

"Sure. I'm too thin to make good stew meat."

"You aren't so far wrong, at that," Kilton said. "About Kobo making stew meat out of you. Many a man has graced his pots."

Patsy repressed a shudder. "I saw Kobo on the trail a few days ago. He looked at me and I felt as though I had been hung up in a butcher shop."

"Is that right?" said Sheridan, sitting up straight. "Kilton, where did your boys come from?"

"I robbed the chain gangs down in the lowlands."

"Then you're pretty much on the outs with Aboo-Tabak, that right?"

Kilton nodded. "Sure. And I'm on the outs with King Kobo. I'm on the outs all the way around, if you ask me."

Sheridan leaned forward, eyes glinting. "But Kobo doesn't watch you very close, does he? Or pay attention to you?"

"No. I don't guess so."

"Then if there isn't any active warfare going on between you and Kobo, it will be all right to solicit his help in this affair, won't it?"

"Sho', now! Kobo isn't going to help anybody!"

"I think he might. Listen, Patsy. Do you know the route to Kobo's camp?"

"Certainly, but I hope you're not thinking of going there tonight!"

"Tonight's as good as any other time, isn't it?"

Patsy regarded him, her mouth pursed thoughtfully. Kilton snorted and reached behind him for a pack of playing cards, which he spread out before him on the cleared board.

"I'd hate to lay odds on your getting away from them alive. Didn't you hear me say something about *Duadillah*?"

Sheridan nodded. "Certainly. But what's a sun god or two among friends?"

Kilton swept up the deck and dealt himself a hand of solitaire. Patsy rose and started piling the dishes on the makeshift kitchen table, scraping them for the brown maid who would come in the morning.

Sheridan smiled at them both and lighted a cigarette. "So you don't think I've got the nerve to walk into Kobo's village and beard him!"

Kilton looked up and tugged at his mustache. "Nerve! Who

said anything about nerve? I've heard enough about you and what you used to do with the Nineteenth Route Army!"

"Well, then," said Sheridan, "if my valor is safe from stain, I suppose I ought to subside. But I'm afraid I can't. You got to talking about Tennessee and all that, and I'd like to see Patsy go back there sometime."

"She will, don't worry about that. Take that lantern and lift that trapdoor and look into the tunnel under the house."

Sheridan shook his head. "I've seen mine tunnels before. And I've heard a lot about wire gold. It pinches out."

Patsy looked around quickly and then went on piling dishes. Kilton frowned, got up. "Let's go outside for some air."

Sheridan followed the man through the door and stopped when Kilton placed his broad, flat hands on the railing.

"What did I do?" asked Sheridan. "Pull a boner?"

"I reckon you did. I don't want Patsy to worry any more about this than she has to. I've been thinking this thing over all day, and the more I think about it, the less chance I think there is of my taking any more gold out of this ledge."

"I'm sorry," said Sheridan.

"Oh, it's all right, no harm done. I said something about it myself this afternoon, before I thought. Listen, Sheridan, have you any money?"

"If I had any, I'd hand it right over. But I haven't."

"Oh, I'm not trying to borrow anything from you. I thought you and Patsy might have a chance to make the coast and swipe your boat if it's still there."

"And leave you?"

"Well, it's this way. I'm a wanted man—there's a price on

my head—and if I went with you the authorities might take in all of us. I couldn't let that happen. Patsy's running a risk being here with me right now. I could stay here and chance it, I guess."

"Not on your life."

Kilton shifted his weight uneasily. "That's all I can think about." He swallowed and changed the subject. "What did you come down here for, anyway?"

Sheridan smiled. "That would be telling."

"Sorry," said Kilton. A light step sounded in the doorway behind them and Kilton reached out a hand toward the horizon, pointing. "Looks like there's going to be right smart of a moon the first thing we know. Ought to be up now."

Patsy came up and laid her hand on Kilton's arm. "What's the matter, Dad? You're holding out on me!"

"Oh! I was just saying that the moon ought to be right pretty tonight."

Sheridan stepped back away from them, looking out across the clearing. His face was in shadow, but his eyes, light gray, glinted like two mother-of-pearl disks in the half-light. "There go the drums again. Still know the way up there, Patsy?"

"Sure now," said Kilton. "You really aren't going to do anything that foolish, are you?" He coughed and looked at Patsy. "Why, those fellas would tie you to a stake and cut you up in no time! Then where would you be?"

"In the pot," said Sheridan. "I don't intend to take Patsy into the camp, but if she knows the trail I think it would be a saving of time if she went with me. Of course, I could follow the sound of the drums, but—"

"I'll go," said Patsy. She went inside, threw back the beaded curtain which led to her room and in a moment they heard her throwing her boots down on the floor, preparatory to dressing in riding clothes.

"I wish you'd believe me," said Kilton. "There isn't any use of your doing that. It's certain death, Sheridan. And if I went with you, these fellas I've got here would take for the jungle in a minute. They're none too staunch with me, and I'm going to need them."

"Patsy won't be in any danger. I'll post her in a tree several yards away from the farthest edge of the village."

"Oh, she can take care of herself all right, I'm not worrying about that. Wait! Look there! Isn't that something moving—?"

A ray of the rising moon struck fire from the tip of a spear. From the porch a ragged ribbon of scarlet sparks ripped through the darkness.

Sheridan listened to the grunt which followed the shot and then put the automatic back in its holster. "Sorry to interrupt you, Kilton, but I thought I'd better throw his aim off." He pointed to the spear, which quivered from a porch upright.

Patsy ran out, hopping, and holding one boot. "What was that?"

"Trying to hit the moon," said Kilton. "You go back and get dressed. Didn't I bring you up any better than that?"

When she had turned away, the two men raced out across the compound and knelt beside the sprawled body. Sheridan raised the head, studied it briefly, then let it thump back against the hard ground. "One of Aboo-Tabak's scouts," he said in a matter-of-fact voice. "Portuguese Joe isn't taking any chances on your getting away before he gets Patsy from you."

"She'll be as safe with you as she will be with me," said Kilton, dusting off the knees of his baggy pants. "Let's haul this thing back under the brush where she won't see it. I'll get a boy to bury it."

Kilton clapped his hands and a shadow trotted toward them—one of his men. "Listen, you," said Kilton. "Bury this after the moon comes up. Right now you get two horses and saddle them and bring them around to the front of the house. Don't stand there with your mouth open, get moving!"

The native blinked. "Hy! You shoot along this fella boy?"

"No, he died of heart failure. Get those horses!"

When the boy had gone, the two went back into the hut and sat down, waiting for Patsy. She came out in a moment, heels rapping the rough planks, hair held in place by a white band. The Luger swung against her side, snub-nosed and businesslike.

"Ready," she said. "Where are the horses?"

The answer came from the front of the hut in the form of a nicker. The boy, silhouetted in the new moonlight, sat down on the step, holding the reins.

"Now don't worry any while we're gone," said Sheridan. "I won't be very long." He reached over and took the cards from the table, pocketing them. Then he lifted the Mannlicher rifle he had taken from the soldier and slung it across his back, crossing it with one of Kilton's Lee-Enfields. From the cartridge cases he loaded a dozen clips and a bandolier with ammunition.

"You look like you're going to war," said Kilton.

"Maybe I am. And if so, I don't want to have to wait until I can see their eye whites because my ammunition's low."

Sheridan clanked outside and held Patsy's stirrup for her. When she had mounted, he swung up on his own mount. The motion was as easy as flowing silk.

"I'll try to breathe while you're gone," said Kilton on the porch. "But if you have to, shoot old Kobo before you bother with the rest of his rats."

"Okay." Sheridan wheeled his horse, drawing rein until Patsy could lead the way. Moonlight sparkled on the crossed rifles as they dived into the jungle trail.

CHAPTER SIX

Triumph Turns to Ashes

THE trail up into the hills was winding, rocky, dangerous because of its sudden twists and abrupt drops. Where they passed through jungle they traveled in a black tunnel and the trail was patterned by moving triangles and squares of yellow, where the trees allowed the moon to filter through. And when they reached a cliffside, the white limestone stood like paralyzed ghosts about them. The black, bottomless caverns dropped away from them. And above them the sky was a white blue, dominated by the smiling disk of the moon. It was light, far too light for Sheridan's comfort.

He spurred up beside Patsy when they reached an edge. Sensing that he wanted to talk, she drew rein.

"Are we almost there?" he asked. "I can hear the drums better now."

"Almost. I'm glad you slacked up."

Sheridan leaned toward her from his saddle, easy and supple. "What do you mean by that? Think old Kobo will get the best of me?"

Two small lines of worry showed against her forehead. "I'm afraid he might, at that."

"But what difference would it make if he did? Difference to you, I mean."

"Let's ride on."

"No, let's sit right here and look at the moon. What difference would it make?"

"Oh, I'd hate to see a white man—any man—hurt on either my father's or my account."

"You're telling fibs. And this moon is bright enough to tell me that."

"Let's ride on."

"And if I were a bold, dashing young man, instead of a paid killer—"

"*Paid* killer?"

Sheridan sank back into his saddle. "Let's ride on."

The horses minced their way down the cliffside and trotted over the level ground. The hill behind them was throwing back the booming, swelling roar of the drums until it hurt their ears.

For ten minutes they pursued their way in silence. Then Patsy drew in. "We'd better leave the horses here. We're within a hundred yards of the camp. When you get this close to the drums, you can't hear them very well."

Sheridan slid off his pony, placed his hands under her arms and helped her down.

Patsy, ducking under the low branches and picking her way through the tangle, was a white blur in the darkness. Sheridan walked soundlessly, but in a moment it was evident that a herd of elephants could have passed that way unheard. The drums shattered the night, rolling, throbbing. They were deafening.

The sight that greeted their eyes was at once horrible and

colorful. A ring of natives, painted every color, masked with every horrible imagining of a witch doctor, faced a leaping fire in the center of the ring. Their feet moved sideways in time to the rolling knuckles of the drummers, and the circle swayed and shifted, making gargantuan shadows against the jungle trees.

Beside the fire, tied to a stake, was a goat, its eyes glazed by the unaccustomed sound, sight and color. This, Sheridan knew, was only the start. But even so, the men were tipsy—quarrelsome with palm whiskey. Occasionally the dancers broke ranks and dipped into the skin buckets which had been placed near at hand. Refreshed, more ugly than ever, they would then return to their places in the circle and dance on.

Patsy, standing in the shadows beside Sheridan, gripped his arm.

Placing his mouth close to her ear, he said, "Climb up that fig tree and watch. If anything happens, you'll have a chance to run. And no one can stumble over you up there."

She shook her head. "I'll take that Lee-Enfield, if you don't mind. And that pocketful of bullets you brought for it. I'll want to be able to shoot fast if they mob you."

"It wouldn't do any good," he protested. But she had already pulled the gun over his head and was inching back to the base of the fig tree.

Her eyes studied Sheridan's face. Then she moved forward, slowly, and very deliberately kissed him on the mouth. Her boots scraped on the bark as she went up.

But even so, the men were tipsy—quarrelsome
with palm whiskey.

Sheridan, blinking, turned again, studying the clearing. A high seat, constructed of hand-hewn boards, had been placed between two trees at one side of the opening. On it sat King Kobo, reeling slightly, gripping a short stick. A brief shiver ran over Sheridan. The head of the stick had appeared to be a round ball some four inches in diameter, but when Kobo turned it, Sheridan saw that the thing was a dried human head, incredibly shrunken.

Other heads were there, hanging from poles, impaled on spikes, sitting in rows on boards.

Sheridan made his way around the outer edge of the circle until he was directly behind Kobo. The drummers, legs crossed before their crude instruments, swayed in time to their own rhythm. On each end of the row sat a man with a buffalo horn, adding an occasional note to the uproar.

Sheridan crept forward until he could touch Kobo's chair. Then, sliding up without a sound, he gained his feet and leaned against the left-hand tree, as though he had been there all evening.

King Kobo, brown, clothed only in a loincloth, raked the circle before him with his eyes, taking in the scene, presiding over it, master of the universe, to judge from the expression on his face. His eyes slanted in Sheridan's direction, started to look away and then jerked back. Kobo's jaw went slack, and the hand that held the headed stick tightened. His black eyes gleamed with both anger and a new idea. He raised his hand to stop the drummers.

Instantly Sheridan turned. He placed his empty palm before Kobo's face. Then he turned it, showing the brown man that nothing was held. Sheridan jerked his wrist, and the two of spades fluttered down into Kobo's lap.

The brown jaw fell, the white filed teeth glittered in the firelight. Unaware that anything was wrong, the dancers danced on, the drummers drummed, stifling all speech.

Sheridan showed the hand to be empty again, turned it carefully. The six of diamonds fluttered out of his empty palm. Kobo leaned back, fear seeping through him, taking the starch out of his spine. Sheridan displayed the entire deck of cards. Then he let them shower down from his right hand to his left. When he opened his left hand the cards were no longer there. Sheridan opened his right hand and exhibited the deck. Kobo twirled his stick, nervous, uncertain.

Pocketing the deck, Sheridan leaned back against the tree and fell to watching the dancers once more. The drummers, their eyes rolling white with ecstasy, filled the clearing with sound.

Kobo spoke. "What for you come along here?"

Turning slowly, Sheridan replied. "Tonight I am going to attack the village. There is much spoil there, many men—Aboo-Tabak. I came to invite you to come along."

"Who with you?"

"No one."

Kobo looked surprised. He glanced anxiously about him into the trees. Such a statement could not be true. "You want me to attack Aboo-Tabak?"

"I want you to attack King Aboo-Tabak."

"Aboo-Tabak not king. I, Kobo, king of this island."

"Aboo-Tabak says that you lie."

Kobo quivered, his face grew sullen. Several of the dancers had looked back to see Sheridan. They sat as if transfixed. But the drummers had not seen. The drumming began once more, louder than before. It was a swelling, rolling sound, unlike that of any civilized drum. It was without cessation, depending for its rhythm upon modulation alone.

The men in the circle got to their feet.

Kobo raised the dried head to them, jerked it toward him. The dancers stalked forward. Sheridan, even though he knew that a fight would occur in the space of seconds, watched them coolly, made no move toward his gun.

The carved wooden masks, nightmare faces, swung forward, wobbling, great eyes cruel. The sharp ceremonial spears were gripped in capable brown hands. The feet shuffled in the dust. The entire line drew straight, curved into a semicircle about the seat and began to close in. The goat, stupefied, pulled at the rope and looked into the fringe of trees.

In the fig tree across the clearing, Sheridan saw a glint of steel. Patsy was up there. Sheridan slowly shook his head and smiled. The drummers, aware now of the impending kill, doubled their volume of sound. The waves of vibration battered against Sheridan's ears like artillery fire, making his eyes ache.

He raised his hand and pointed at the goat. It kicked suddenly, fell over on its side and lay still. Kobo stared. He did not know that Sheridan, taking advantage of the sound, had shot from the hip with his left gun.

Sheridan, even though he knew that a fight would occur
in the space of seconds, watched them coolly,
made no move toward his gun.

But it was too late to stop the line. In the center a giant mask bobbed nearer, swaying. It encased the head of Kobo's medicine man.

Sheridan sighed through tight throat muscles. His trick with the goat had failed. He had waited too long. The first of the dancers was less than ten feet away from him—and that first was the medicine man.

Abruptly the great mask jerked. The legs below it caved. The witch doctor pitched forward on his face, the wooden casque rolling up to Sheridan's feet. A round hole appeared in the back. Sheridan had seen the flame dart from the fig tree, but the others had not. The sound of the Lee-Enfield had been drowned in the roaring of the drums.

The line stopped, stood motionless for the space of fifteen seconds. Then a man moved back. Another moved. Still another. Suddenly the ranks broke. Natives scattered away like a flock of startled blackbirds, sprawling in their haste.

Sheridan picked up the wooden mask and put it on the crook of his arm. He did not want Kobo to see the bullet hole.

Kobo had shrunk, his eyes staring. The dried head had fallen to the ground. In a weak voice, Kobo said, "You attack this Aboo-Tabak tonight?"

"Are you coming with me?"

"But night is night and devils walk. This is *Duadillah*, even though."

"Then you're afraid of Aboo-Tabak."

"No. Only of *Duadillah*."

"But Aboo-Tabak goes out at night to fight."

Kobo sat forward. "Yes, but he got a charm—charm on his

chest. Round face shines in the night. Talks. Aboo-Tabak not afraid with that charm."

Once more Sheridan sighed. He knew that Kobo referred to the luminous-dialed alarm clock Aboo-Tabak wore.

"If I get you a charm like that tonight, will you attack Aboo-Tabak and the town?"

Kobo nodded vigorously. "Sure. Plenty fight."

"All right," said Sheridan. "I will bring you a charm before morning. I am going now to get one."

Sheridan strode across the clearing, past the fire, and into the darkness which lay beyond. When he was out of Kobo's sight, he circled back to the base of the fig tree. He was about to whistle when his foot struck something soft at the base.

Puzzled, he stooped and reached out. A naked shoulder, wet and sticky, met his fingers. In sudden fear he jerked the thing into a sitting position. The head lolled back. Enough firelight reached this point to show that the jaw was gone. The eyes were already hard.

Sheridan stared up into the tree. He whistled hopefully. No sound came back to him. He called in a low voice, but still there was no response.

Returning his attention to the dead man, Sheridan studied what was left of the face. Judging from the ugly features, this was one of Aboo-Tabak's men from the lowlands. And if this were true . . .

Searching with swift fingers through the grass, Sheridan found the rifle. He jerked back the bolt and pumped out the cartridges, counting them. Two were missing. Eyes narrow, he looked back at the fire.

The story was plain enough to him now. He and Patsy had been trailed and lost. Aboo-Tabak's men had seen the powder flame when Patsy fired the first shot at the witch doctor. They had climbed the tree and dragged her down. But she had shot one of them, and the sound had been muffled by the last rumble of the drums before they stopped altogether.

Then they had taken Patsy. Where was she now? Had they refrained from killing her in anger when she had shot that man?

Sheridan's heart pounded, like the accelerating tempo of a shaken clock. Like the clock he had to find before he could make the second move.

CHAPTER SEVEN

Holy Ben Gets a Warning

LEADING Patsy's horse, Sheridan galloped headlong down the crooked trails toward Kilton's mine. The moon was brighter than before, giving the world a pearly brilliance. The black depths and the white heights went by, disregarded.

Sheridan was ready for anything—and anything might happen. Aboo-Tabak's men knew that he ranged the jungle, and they would be on the lookout for him, but they would exercise great caution in attacking him. Sheridan knew that. They had seen his ability with a gun demonstrated too many times.

Ahead a greenish light appeared through the trees, a light eerie and bordering upon the supernatural. It was like the eye of an idol, cold and lusterless. Sheridan drew rein and the horse he led thumped against the other's flank with a startled snort. Sheridan proceeded slowly, watching the green light. Then he relaxed. It was nothing more than a rotten stump impregnated with phosphorus.

He swung down and approached it on foot. The punk wood sparkled and glowed, died out and flared again. With a half smile he scooped up a handful of the luminous damp material and thrust it into his trousers pocket. Mounting again, he spurred his horse into a gallop.

The sound of rifle fire was in the air, far away, like the

crackle of a fire or the wholesale snapping of twigs. Sheridan drew in once more and placed the direction. With a suddenly sinking heart he realized that the mine was being attacked.

The dull, hollow reports of the Lee-Enfield were becoming better defined. Yells interspersed the occasional volleys from the sharp Mannlichers. Hopefully, Sheridan listened for a thundering Luger, or for a second Lee-Enfield, but the sound was not forthcoming. It meant, then, that Sorry Kilton was making the fight alone.

Sheridan's first impulse was to smash through the besieging circle to help Kilton keep them off, but he realized that the plan, however gallant, was not good sense. He had to remain on the loose, in the hope of soliciting Kobo's legions of brown spearmen. And he had to find Patsy before anything happened to her—providing nothing had happened as yet.

Tying his horses to a mango tree, he proceeded swiftly on foot. The shooting was growing in volume. Twice Sheridan saw brown shadows flit across the trail before him, but he did not fire or otherwise give any inkling of his presence. They would know soon enough that he was here.

A bullet snapped through leaves over his head and he ducked before he realized that it was a random shot, probably from Kilton's rifle.

Abruptly the jungle fell away from him. In the bright moonlight he could see the hut in the center of the compound. A trunk was across the doorway, and over the top of the trunk came spurts of flame.

While he stood there, the firing in the jungle fell off. That meant but one thing. The men of Aboo-Tabak were preparing for a charge against the hut.

Simultaneously a dozen brown shadows dashed out of the edge of the jungle. Greasy skin shimmered in the moonlight. The spears glittered like mirrors. From a hundred throats came a war cry.

Sheridan stepped out into the compound, in plain sight, his white clothes making him a perfect target. Both automatics leaped into his palms. His eyes were chill, his lips drawn back away from his flashing teeth. Feet planted far apart, he cracked down on the man nearest the hut. The man shrieked and fell back.

Before the echo of that shot had died away, the second Polynesian stumbled and skidded to a quivering stop in the dirt. Sheridan's hands moved up and down like well-oiled piston rods, firing with a sure, deliberate rhythm. Before the attack was even well started, five sprawling men were like empty black sacks against the moonlit ground.

The shouts in the jungle died. Natives hugged the dirt, suddenly afraid. Their wild glances centered on Sheridan's white figure. But before a rifle could be raised, Sheridan was gone. And before order had come out of the sudden chaos, he had mounted his pony and was galloping toward the sea.

He knew that they would not try another attack until they were quite certain that he was no longer there. And that would take at least two hours of search. If they would only hold back that long, there was a chance that he could bring up the forces of Kobo in time.

But before he could do that he had to find a clock. The humor of it brought a dry chuckle to his lips, though his eyes did not smile. He was betting two, perhaps three lives against a ticking timepiece worth no more than a dollar. And from what Sorry Kilton had said, the chest that had been stolen had contained two hundred thousand dollars and considerably more. . . .

Far ahead of him, shimmering through the trees below, the ocean lay calm and serene beneath the caress of the moon, but he rode too fast to see the beauty of it. He was wondering whether or not they had found the other horse. If they had, they might think that he was still back there near the hut. If they thought that . . .

Sheridan avoided the town. He headed for the water's edge and dismounted in the shadow of the overhanging palms. For several minutes he searched along the littered sand and then, with a smile of satisfaction, he came back to his horse, mounted and rode into the village.

Several lights flickered along the streets, and a hurricane lantern guttered before the trading post. Sheridan swung down before the door and tramped up the steps, eyes alert, hands brushing the guns on his thighs.

Charles Wesley Witherspoon glanced up from the makeshift desk at the far end of the smelly, cluttered place. He peered over the edge of his rimless glasses, adjusted them hurriedly and stared again. His greasy singlet clung damply to his ribs. A fat, flabby hand darted to the drawer.

A stubby automatic appeared in Sheridan's palm. "I wouldn't, if I were you."

"Wouldn't what?" queried Witherspoon innocently. Nevertheless he laid his palms flat down on the desktop and remained peering over the rims of his spectacles. "If you're thinking about that check now, I had to give it to Portu— I mean *Governador* Batista."

"Never mind the check, it isn't any good anyway. I'm here for some information."

Witherspoon repressed a hiccup. "Ask away," he said airily.

Sheridan moved until his back was away from the entrance. "Has anyone come into town for the last hour?"

"Only yourself, guv'nor, only yourself. They all left here a right good while ago. Wanted me to go along, they did. Said I could have some business if I went. But I figured I'd better not. Been pretty far behind in my bookkeeping, y'see."

"Then in that case I'll give you a little tip. Kobo is going to be on the rampage before morning. You'd better lock up and hit for the hills."

"Lord! Is he now!"

"You don't happen to have any clocks here, do you?"

"Sure now, guv'nor, what could anybody want with a clock in this place?"

"Listen, Holy Ben. Have you buried anyone in the last twenty-four hours?"

"And who would I bury? Of course, Cap'n Sheridan, a whole stack of natives have died, but I don't get business burying them. These fellas along the coast are all Mohammedans—infidels, so to speak. They do their own burying."

"Quit stalling! I've often wondered how a bullet would sound going through a fat man."

"Sure now!" whined Witherspoon. "You wouldn't shoot me, would you?"

"What do *you* think? Listen, Holy Ben. Trying to keep me here until somebody comes in that door isn't going to do you a bit of good. I know there's big money waiting for you if you get me. But if anyone comes in that door, you'll get the first bullet, even before I turn around!"

"Ow! Listen, Cap'n! I buried a fella just before dark. I'll even take you up there and show you the grave. But by hell, get out of here, quick!"

Sheridan spun on his heel and tramped down the steps to his horse. Holy Ben Witherspoon was slumped over his desk.

Across the street, outside Batista's office, a Portuguese sentry dozed, head on his drawn-up knees. His rifle lay beside him on the ground, glinting in the moonlight. Sheridan rode on by and picked out the trail that would lead up to Kobo's stronghold in the mountains.

Jungle birds raised sleepy protest at the rapid clatter of horse's hoofs on the moon-drenched trail.

CHAPTER EIGHT

Sheridan's Answer to Dynamite

KOBO'S hillmen had resumed their dance, but the ceremony had taken on a different tone. This was no longer for the benefit of *Duadillah*—this was in preparation for war. The ceremonial spears had been replaced by the uglier, shorter weapons of warfare, and the flames leaped from the logs and threw red fire against the naked metal and naked bodies until the entire scene seemed to drip with blood.

The ring of warriors swayed and howled, their voices drowned by the drums. Kobo, silver-mounted pistol thrust in the belt of his loincloth, sat erect and fierce upon his throne, waiting.

Sheridan slipped through the jungle until he reached the clearing. Then, walking deliberately, he made his way toward Kobo.

Kobo's black eyes were eager as they watched Sheridan's approach. The headed stick bobbed and the drums stopped. The dancers turned, watching.

"The charm?" hissed Kobo.

Sheridan stood before him. From his pocket he drew two disks and held them up. "I bring two, not one. You will be doubly protected against *Duadillah* and the warriors of Aboo-Tabak."

Kobo stared at the objects. The faces of the disks glowed

71

with a sullen green light. Kobo stretched forth his hand and took them. He pressed each in turn against his ear. His features lighted.

"They speak!" he whispered with awe.

"They speak," repeated Sheridan. "Louder even than Aboo-Tabak's charm. But if you are not victorious tonight they will speak no longer. And if you fail to do my bidding, their power will turn against you."

Kobo regarded the glowing disks with respect. To each a cord was attached. He quickly tied them around his neck and stood up. The disks knocked together. Their ticking could be heard in the dead silence.

"*Ai!*" cried Kobo. "*Ke marfik!* Look alive! We go to the house of the white man with the hairy face. We go to attack Aboo-Tabak, to kill his followers. There will be spoils and meat!"

A swelling shout followed the words.

Sheridan mounted his horse and listened to the noise Kobo's men made in leaving. Then he spurred ahead, ducking low to avoid the branches, and galloped toward the mine.

A hundred yards from the clearing edge, Sheridan stopped and dismounted. He feared for the worst. They had obviously overwhelmed Kilton, perhaps they had put him to death. Sheridan had more than one reason for hating that thought.

Walking on the balls of his feet, he approached the hut. At the clearing edge he stopped, listening. The silence was electric, unnatural. Something was wrong, more than wrong. Somewhere eyes were watching his white body at the jungle's edge.

The moon above was serene, sailing along its course attended by its court of small fleecy clouds. A palm frond stirred, rattling. A lizard chirped dismally. A bird fluttered its wings and settled back in sleep. The hut, alone and silent, gave no clue to any danger.

Sheridan stepped forward, balanced, hands near his guns. The rifle across his back swung easily.

A head appeared behind him. Another head. A white figure jumped out of the door of the hut and cried, "Take him!"

Yowls burst from a hundred throats. A dozen rifles barked. A swarm of men, hardly more than a bulky shadow, rounded the end of the hut and raced toward Sheridan.

Sheridan swore. They had been waiting for him, knowing that he would come back. And they had caught him flat-footed.

The blue steel of his automatic shimmered. Smashing ribbons of powder sparks ripped away from his waist. The man nearest him fell back, shrieking. Sheridan stepped away, rapidly. Rifles roared at him. He fired again, looking wildly toward the hut to find Portuguese Joe.

Abruptly the jungle burst apart. The roar doubled, trebled in volume. Kobo had arrived.

War clubs splintered war clubs. Spears sang against spears. Men went down like ninepins—Aboo-Tabak's men, unable to gain their wits in time. The clearing was a milling black horde, blurred with action, blasted with yells. The lowland natives fell away, screaming. Kobo, two disks glowing on his chest, smashed his way through the thick of the mob, a towering figure. Portuguese Joe was not to be seen.

As suddenly as it had begun it was ended. Men lay squirming

and groaning in the dirt. Others leaned against palms, heads drooping, exhausted. Still others sprawled in dark pools, never to move again.

Sheridan was breathing hard. He knew that this was not the end of the struggle. Aboo-Tabak and Portuguese Joe were not there. And Kobo had made a circular attack. It would have been impossible for Aboo-Tabak and Portuguese Joe to escape. And Sheridan had a feeling that Patsy was somewhere near.

A voice, shrill and whining, came out of the hut. "Sheridan!" It was Portuguese Joe. "I have Kilton here. And I have this girl. If you do not give me safe conduct, *senhor,* I will kill them both!"

Sheridan straightened and stared at the hut. He walked to the porch, standing out of sight of the door, his reloaded guns ready. "To hell with that bluff! Come out here, or I'll come in!"

Something sputtered through the air, landing in the clearing, showering sparks. Sheridan jumped back, covering his face. A terrific roar thundered through the jungle. Sheridan staggered under the impact of the concussion.

Portuguese Joe was using Kilton's dynamite! And Portuguese Joe, Aboo-Tabak, Patsy and Kilton were down there in the mine tunnel. It would be impossible to assault that stronghold. And it would be impossible to keep Kobo and his men here more than a few hours.

Sheridan looked about him. On the far side of the clearing stood the toolshed, filled with its mining equipment. With a half prayer on his lips, Sheridan ran toward it.

The door was locked, but a bullet through the keyhole remedied that. Sheridan entered the dim interior, feeling about with his hands. First he encountered a small, portable gasoline engine. Then he found a round barrel. Dragging the object to light, he examined it.

It was a portable diamond drill, weighing less than four hundred pounds complete. As good an engineer as Kilton would hardly mine without one. Sheridan fixed a four-foot drill bit into the snout of the hammer and started the gasoline engine.

"What you got?" Kobo demanded from the doorway, distrustfully eyeing the sputtering engine.

"Magic," Sheridan said, dragging the machine into the moonlight.

"Good magic?" demanded Kobo.

"Good magic."

Sheridan eyed the strike of the rock ribs which peeped through the soil. Then he estimated the dip of any vein. With Kobo's help he pulled the machine into the shadow behind the house.

"Portuguese Joe!" shouted Sheridan. "I've got a machine gun here and I'm going to splinter that trapdoor. If you so much as touch the Kiltons, I'll treat you as I treated the datto in the Malay States."

Sheridan sank the bit of the drill into the soil and pulled the trigger. The machine shook in his hands. It was almost the same thing that contractors use in tearing up streets, and its chattering sound was louder than a riveter's.

The series of one-inch holes in the ground grew into a half

circle, three-quarters of a circle. And the moon passed through the greater part of an hour's arc. Then Sheridan stopped the engine and laid the drill aside. He heard Portuguese Joe's laugh from the interior of the hut.

Sheridan gripped the two automatics. He stood back, aware of Kobo's mystified eyes. Sheridan jumped squarely into the middle of the ring of holes.

It seemed to Kobo that the ground opened and swallowed the white man completely and Kobo drew away, his teeth chattering with fear, gripping the two luminous disks which hung about his throat.

Sheridan had guessed right. He had drilled into the center of the mine tunnel. He landed in a shower of dirt and dust, struggling to keep his feet.

Portuguese Joe was standing at the bottom of the ladder that led to the floor of the hut, looking up, his hands gripping a rifle. At the sound of the falling dirt he whirled about, uttering a hoarse cry—to confront Sheridan's guns.

Aboo-Tabak whipped a knife from his belt and jumped forward. Sheridan fired, and the knife went spinning away. Kilton, bound, tried to grin. Patsy, disheveled, struggled to get to her feet.

Portuguese Joe sagged down to his knees with a jerk, lifting the rifle, but a well-aimed kick from Kilton's foot destroyed his aim. Sheridan walked forward, slowly, confident. "Sorry to break in on you folks this way, but wasn't this party down here getting a little rough?"

Portuguese Joe's eyes were like poached eggs. Aboo-Tabak licked dry lips.

Disarming the pair, Sheridan transferred Kilton's ropes to them. Patsy, numb with relief, gazed up at Sheridan with tearful eyes.

"You'd make a pretty good mining engineer," was Kilton's only comment. He was busy hoisting Portuguese Joe up the ladder and into the hut.

Patsy climbed the ladder, regained her gun and walked out on the porch, staring at the group of prisoners which were held by Kobo's men. When Sheridan came up to her, she whispered, "I knew you'd come for us."

But Sorry Kilton was all business. His mustache bristled. "All right, you greasy baboon. What did you do with that chest you stole from me?"

"I won't tell you."

Sheridan drew out a pocketknife and felt of its edge. But Portuguese Joe only cowered back.

"I won't tell you!" he whined.

Sheridan shrugged. "I don't want to cut him up, and I don't think it's necessary, Kilton. We'll all go down to the village."

"The village?"

"Sure. And from there we'll board my sloop and sail back to Shanghai."

"Shanghai!" exclaimed Kilton. "What do you mean?"

"What I said. Shanghai. Kilton, I was sent down here to kill you and take your dead body back there."

"Then . . . then . . ." said Patsy, "you're just a . . . a paid killer!"

"I'm not getting any pay for this, Patsy. I'm protecting my own neck. You see, a couple of months ago I sold the Chinese army some shells from a US firm. Unknown to me, the shells didn't have any powder in them. Only sand. The penalty for that is death."

"Then what are we going to do?" wailed Patsy.

"Let me finish down in the village," Sheridan replied.

CHAPTER NINE

A Last Spear for a Last Man

IT was a glum walk down to the sea. The prisoners had been pressed into service as porters, taking Kilton's belongings with them. And Aboo-Tabak's eyes were uncomfortable on the back of Portuguese Joe's neck. Kilton made no effort at resistance and Patsy rode silently ahead, glancing at Sheridan occasionally, disappointment in her face.

When they reached the cemetery, they stopped. From down the hill came the sound of footsteps, and in a few minutes Charles Wesley Witherspoon was with them.

Sheridan eyed him. "Glad you came up here."

"Thought maybe there was some business for me," replied Holy Ben. "Saw all this mob and thought—"

"Yes, there was a fight— And a good one. You remember what I asked you about burying anybody today?"

Holy Ben glanced distrustfully at Portuguese Joe and then, understanding that Portuguese Joe's reign was over, smiled back at Sheridan and seated himself on the cemetery wall.

"The fifth grave from this end," said Witherspoon. "Pretty heavy coffin it was, too. Took about ten natives to carry it."

Sheridan called for Kobo, and spears were pressed into service as shovels. While they were digging, Sheridan took the alarm clock from about the neck of Aboo-Tabak. Approaching

Kobo, Sheridan removed the two glowing disks in spite of protest and put the alarm clock in their place.

Kobo grinned. He seemed pleased.

Sheridan began to speak to no one in particular. "I hate to have to take a man back to those Shanghai devils."

"Undoubtedly," said Patsy bitterly.

"But it wasn't any fault of mine. I had to do this to save my own neck. They told me if I brought Kilton back, they'd reinstate me and forget about the black sand. Before I came down here I scouted around a good bit and found out a few things."

One of the spears struck the surface of the "coffin." Natives struggled down into the hole. It took a round dozen of them to lift the chest out. Sheridan rose and pried off the lid. The moon sparkled on much better than two hundred thousand dollars in gold bullion. Sheridan waved a careless hand at it and closed the lid again. Portuguese Joe grunted uncomfortably. Aboo-Tabak half rose, then sank back again.

"Now to go on with my story," said Sheridan. "Before I came down here, I did quite a bit of investigating. I heard about Portuguese Joe setting himself up as governor. I knew who he was. And I heard all about that Solomon Island business.

"Kilton, they didn't let it out that you'd robbed a bank. They didn't say anything to anybody except me. They wanted to make you believe that, and they wanted me to believe that. But let me tell you something. They cooked up all this to drive you out of the deal, Kilton. And they want you back again dead—and only dead—because they don't want to have to share this Solomon Island wealth with you.

"After you disappeared, Kilton, driven away by their threats, they sold that property in the Solomon Islands for a cool million. And as soon as they got your dead body in their hands, they were going to cook up a default on your part. But half of that million is still yours. And all of this two hundred thousand is yours.

"That's why they lied to you, Kilton. And that's why they sent me down here to kill you. They thought they had me under their thumb. As a matter of fact, they couldn't get a man in Shanghai to take this task. Everyone knows your reputation with a gun. So they framed me, and then told me that I'd have to kill you to get my name clear.

"That's the setup, Kilton, and if we cruise back up there and walk into their offices, their fat little clerks will shake in their chairs and they'll fork over without a squawk. And if I want to be reinstated, they'll have to reinstate me."

Kilton had stood up. Suddenly he reached out and grabbed Sheridan's hand. "God bless you, boy!" he said.

Patsy was beaming. She was about to approach Sheridan when a sudden movement diverted her attention.

Portuguese Joe, driven wild by Aboo-Tabak's glance, leaped to his feet and raced across the moonlit cemetery, shrieking.

Aboo-Tabak sprang up. A spear was lying at his feet. He snatched it up, balanced himself, and threw it with all the skill at his command.

Portuguese Joe faltered. The shaft went halfway through

him. He slumped forward and shoved the point against the ground, clawing at it. The impact drove the shaft back through. He jerked and lay still, glassy eyes staring up at the moon.

Aboo-Tabak sat down amid the silence which followed the throw. He made a motion as though he dusted his hands. Kobo was beside him and Kobo patted Aboo-Tabak's shoulder. They looked at each other and smiled.

Charles Wesley Witherspoon trotted forward to the crumpled body and knelt beside it, frisking it expertly. Then he removed the spear and pulled the remains toward the hole where the chest had been.

With the moonlight shining upon his bald head, he cleared his throat and said, "Let's see, now. By the Father and the Son and the Holy Ghost . . ."

Kilton looked about him, trying to spot Sheridan. Instead, he saw the natives talking together in low tones. Aboo-Tabak and Kobo were segregating their flocks, preparatory to quitting the place.

Sheridan and Patsy were walking down the hill toward the quay. Kilton heard Sheridan say, "No, I'm not interested in going back into the Chinese army. Not a bit of it. Your dad's got me all hepped up about Tennessee. And I think maybe you and I . . ."

Kilton stroked his mustache and listened for a moment to the droning voice of Charles Wesley Witherspoon.

"I wonder," murmured Kilton, "who put that spear in front of Aboo-Tabak?"

There wasn't any answer, except, perhaps, Holy Ben's voice.

Story Preview

Story Preview

NOW that you've just ventured through one of the captivating tales in the Stories from the Golden Age collection by L. Ron Hubbard, turn the page and enjoy a preview of *All Frontiers Are Jealous*. Join American engineer Dan Courtney as he attempts to survey a railway route through the jungles of central Africa only to be sidetracked when he discovers that an alluring American woman has been kidnapped by the fearsome Dinka warrior tribe. But the plot thickens when he attempts to rescue her and stumbles headlong into a diamond smuggling operation, and the perpetrators want Courtney out of the picture—permanently.

All Frontiers Are Jealous

A few months ago there appeared in the London *Times* a financial notice. The bankers saw nothing unusual about it. The public paid it little heed. Investors shied. A few brokers smiled. Only a few knew the undiluted hell which backed those dry, crisp lines.

SUDAN RAILWAY
TRIED AGAIN

Colonel Malone Asks Aid in
Long-Abandoned Project

Mombasa, Kenya, EEA, March 6 (RS)—Rumors of yet another effort to link the Uganda Railway with the Anglo-Egyptian Railroad were confirmed here by Colonel B. A. Malone, well-known promoter.

Investors will remember the disaster of former ventures when all attempts to survey the line failed.

Colonel Malone, according to his statement, will utilize a short franchise granted him to survey the line. He will attempt to float a loan on the London market.

The only memorandum made concerning this item was handed out to outer-office clerks and read, "No matter what price offered, we are not to be bothered with SR bonds."

However, down in Mombasa and shortly in Nairobi, Colonel Malone grew expansive and hopeful as always. Optimism sprouted from him like green bamboo shoots. He had won and lost half a dozen fortunes but no incident in his life had ever dimmed his winning, if gold-plated smile.

Railroads made money. Colonel Malone made railroads. He had shot his quota of lions at Tsavo. He had sunk his pick into the clay of Tanganyika. He could wave his hand at a map and truthfully say that the thing would be a blank if he hadn't helped matters with railroads.

And, that hot and depressing afternoon, when he alighted at Nairobi in company with a weather-beaten young giant, he ran true to form by saying:

"When I first saw this place, Dan, it was ten mud huts and a sheet-iron shed. Look at it now! Modern. Electric lights! Streets. A post office! We did that with the Uganda Railway. She's a beaut, isn't she, what?"

Dan Courtney glanced at the stubby, wood-burning engine which was panting wearily after its run. He listened for a moment to the yapping roar of the natives in third class.

"Yeah," said Dan Courtney, "she's a beaut."

"And the first thing you know," said Colonel Malone, "the fetid green of jungle and the golden sands of desert will be caressed with the steel highway into the north. Think of it, Dan!"

"Yeah," said Dan. He raised his khaki sun hat and mopped at his brow and gazed longingly down the blazing street at a veranda which looked cool.

"In chains," whispered Malone, ecstatically. "Like a mighty beast, the Dark Continent growls and snarls at us, but within the decade the last link between the Mediterranean and the Indian Ocean will be welded. Progress, Dan, what?"

"Yeah. But I'm not in the market for stock in it. Let's get us a drink of lemon pop or something."

Malone's smile grew sad. "You've no imagination, Dan. No imagination. But then . . . no American ever had an imagination. Leave that and empire to the British, what?"

"Lemonade," persisted the weathered giant. "I got to work the rest of the day."

"Look here," said Malone, "you're not getting cold feet, are you?"

Dan looked down at the heat waves which shivered off the concrete around his scorched boots and grinned.

"You're not going to back out, are you? Look here, Dan, you can't do that! Just because those damned Dinkas murdered Stephans and slaughtered Lawry's men. . . . You wouldn't let that stop *you*, would you, Dan?"

"Who said anything about quitting? A job is a job. I've got to stretch a line from Lake Salisbury and the Uganda to the Anglo-Egyptian at Sennar across the Sudan. I've got to review Lawry's work and confirm his passes and grades and take a blank out of the map in the Dinka country. For that I get three hundred bucks a month and five hundred in stock. It's a job. Let's find some lemonade."

They turned toward the street, starting to thrust their way through the press of natives about the station. But they did not get very far. Two white men of burly build stood in the way and seemed to have heard Dan's last remark. One was short and wide, the other was tall and wide. This last had a narrow head on which two very small, pointed ears were set. One of these ears was half gone. The smaller one's nose took up twice as much territory as it should have and his eyes took up only half their allotted space.

"If it ain't Malone," said the bigger man.

The colonel's pleasant expression hardened like concrete. "Hello, Gotch-ear. I see the local authorities are asleep as usual."

"He kids all the time just like that, Bart," said Gotch-ear to his short friend. "Did I hear Salisbury to Sennar, Malone?"

"That missing chunk don't seem to hurt your hearing any," growled the colonel.

"This tall boy making a safari up by Alak?" persisted Gotch-ear.

"I'll take a safari over your frame if you don't get out of my way," snapped the colonel.

"You wouldn't be thinking of tagging us, would you, big guy?"

"I pick clean trail when I travel, whatever-the-hell-your-name-is," said Dan.

"A Yank," said Gotch-ear. "Listen, big guy, keep your eye on your transit up north. I don't take nothin' from punks, see? And if this is one of your sneaks, Malone, we'll send you back your pal's head in a big wicker basket."

Gotch-ear and Bart moved off into the swarm of natives and were lost. Dan, with a singleness of purpose which was very characteristic of him, headed for the veranda and the cold drink.

"I fired him off the South African road," explained Malone. "He was stealing supplies and selling them. Wonder what the hell he's doing in Nairobi."

"From his looks, it isn't legal," said Dan. "He's jittery."

"Must be important. Gotch-ear's got a nose for money. Wonder why he made a point of heading you off."

"Jittery, that's all," said Dan. "Forget it. Northern Uganda is big enough for a dozen Gotch-ears."

"I wonder if he's being paid to block this road," puzzled Malone, trying to keep up with Dan's long stride and half running to do it in spite of the heat.

"Nuts," said Dan. "All you need is this survey, the franchise and the cash. You'll have the first two and you'll get the third, won't you?"

"The cash?" blinked Malone. "Oh . . . oh yes, of course. Sure I'll get it. I'll float a bond issue on the London market. Sure, that's easy. They'll snap up the SR paper like it was printed on platinum."

A tall and dignified native stepped out from the questionable shade of a warehouse and accosted Dan with great ceremony.

"You look well, *bwana*."

"Hello, Petey," said Dan. "Been having good luck?"

"No, *bwana*."

"Maybe I'll change it for you. Scout out and round up the boys you wired me you had. We scurry out of here this afternoon."

"Yes, *bwana*," said Petey, withdrawing with another bow.

Dan slid into a chair beside a veranda table, pulled off his helmet and fanned lazily at his moist face.

"As soon as I get the equipment together," said Dan, presently, "I'll take that train to the end of the line at Soroti. I want to be well into the country when the rains start."

"You bet you do," said Malone. "You've got eight months to run the line and that's not half enough time. My . . . er . . . ah . . . franchise runs out at that time, you know."

"The bonus of two grand still sticks?"

"Of course. Africa . . ."

Dan didn't listen to the colonel. His attention had been distracted by a very soft and lovely voice at the next table. He squared around slightly, and instantly the lazy boredom froze on his face.

He did not know the girl, but he knew he would very shortly. He had never seen his destiny so plain before him.

To find out more about *All Frontiers Are Jealous* and how you can obtain your copy, go to www.goldenagestories.com.

Glossary

Glossary

STORIES FROM THE GOLDEN AGE *reflect the words and expressions used in the 1930s and 1940s, adding unique flavor and authenticity to the tales. While a character's speech may often reflect regional origins, it also can convey attitudes common in the day. So that readers can better grasp such cultural and historical terms, uncommon words or expressions of the era, the following glossary has been provided.*

Anglo-Egyptian: Anglo-Egyptian Sudan was the name of Sudan between 1899 and 1956, when it was jointly ruled by the United Kingdom and Egypt (which was then under British influence).

Banda Sea: the sea of the south Moluccas (a group of about one hundred and fifty islands) in Indonesia, technically part of the Pacific Ocean but separated from it by the islands.

bandolier: a broad belt worn over the shoulder by soldiers and having a number of small loops or pockets for holding cartridges.

beard: boldly confront or challenge (someone formidable).

blackbirded: engaged in the slave trade, especially in the Pacific.

bob: shilling; a coin used in the United Kingdom worth one-twentieth of a pound.

bolo: a large cutting tool similar to the machete, used particularly in the jungles of Indonesia, the Philippines and in the sugar fields of Cuba. The primary use for the bolo is clearing vegetation, whether for agriculture or during trail blazing.

carpet, pulling you on the: variation of "to call on the carpet"; censure severely or angrily.

casque: a piece of defensive or ornamental armor for the head and neck.

chain gang: a group of prisoners chained together to perform menial or physically challenging labor.

Cosmoline: a substance obtained from the residues of the distillation of petroleum, essentially the same as Vaseline, but of heavy grade. Used as a protective coating for firearms, metals, etc.

datto: Malay tribal chieftain.

Dinka: cattle-herding people of the Nile basin in southern Sudan. The men are warriors and guardians of the camp against predators: lions, hyenas and other enemy raiders.

dip: in mining and geology, the downward slope of a layer of rock or vein.

drill: a strong, twilled cotton fabric.

EEA: Equatorial East Africa; the region of eastern Africa near the equator, primarily including Kenya and northern Tanzania.

G-men: government men; agents of the Federal Bureau of Investigation.

governador: (Portuguese) governor.

Gulliver in Lilliput: refers to a satire, *Gulliver's Travels,* by Jonathan Swift in 1726. Lemuel Gulliver, an Englishman, travels to exotic lands, including Lilliput (where the people are six inches tall), Brobdingnag (where the people are seventy feet tall), and the land of the Houyhnhnms (where horses are the intelligent beings, and humans, called Yahoos, are mute brutes of labor).

hepped: greatly interested.

Java Sea: a shallow sea, formed as sea levels rose at the end of the last ice age, that lies between the Indonesian islands of Borneo and Java.

Lee-Enfield: a standard bolt-action magazine-fed repeating rifle; the British Army's standard rifle for over sixty years from 1895 until 1956, although it remained in British service well into the early 1960s and is still found in service in the armed forces of some Commonwealth nations.

light out: to leave quickly; depart hurriedly.

line, the: the equator.

Luger: a German semiautomatic pistol introduced before World War I and named after German firearms expert George Luger (1849–1923).

Malay States: the Federated Malay States; a federation of four protected states in the Malay Peninsula consisting of Selangor, Perak, Negeri Sembilan and Pahang. It was established by the British government in 1895 and lasted until 1946, it now forms part of Malayasia.

Mannlicher: a type of rifle equipped with a manually operated sliding bolt for loading cartridges for firing, as opposed to the more common rotating bolt of other rifles. Mannlicher rifles were considered reasonably strong and accurate.

massa: (chiefly in southern US) master.

Mombasa: the second largest city in Kenya, lying on the Indian Ocean. In 1894 the British government declared a protectorate over Kenya, calling it the East African Protectorate. In 1901 the first railway line was completed from Mombasa to Kisumu, a city in the southwestern part of Kenya.

Nairobi: the capital and largest city of Kenya in the south central part of the country. Founded in 1899, it became the seat of government for British East Africa in 1905 and capital of independent Kenya in 1963.

pannikin: a small metal drinking cup.

pipe-clayed: clean and smart; pipe clay is a fine white clay used in whitening leather. It was at one time largely used by soldiers for making their gloves, accouterments and clothes look clean and smart.

pith helmet: a lightweight hat made from dried pith, the soft spongelike tissue in the stems of most flowering plants. Pith helmets are worn in tropical countries for protection from the sun.

Polynesian: a native or inhabitant of Polynesia, a large grouping of over 1,000 islands scattered over the central and southern Pacific Ocean.

por Dios: (Spanish) for God's sake.

Princess Pat manual: a rifle drill associated with Princess Patricia's Canadian Light Infantry regiment (named after a member of the British Royal Family, a granddaughter of Queen Victoria). A manual is a prescribed series of movements made with a rifle or other military item, as during a drill or as part of a ceremony.

pull a boner: make a blunder.

punk wood: wood that is decayed.

ragtag, bobtail: the lowest social class; the rabble.

rib: a vein of ore in rock.

Route Army, Nineteenth: a type of military organization, in the Chinese Republic, that consisted of two or more corps or a large number of divisions or independent brigades. The Nineteenth Route Army defended Shanghai during a short war (January 18, 1932 to March 3, 1932) between the armies of the Republic of China and the Empire of Japan.

RS: Reuters Service, the world news and information organization; in October 1851, Paul Julius Reuter (1816–1899), a German-born immigrant, opened an office in the city of London that transmitted stock market quotations between London and Paris. Reuters, as the agency soon became known, eventually extended its service to the whole British press as well as to other European countries. It also expanded the content to include general and economic news from all around the world.

run-over: of boots, where the heel is so unevenly worn on the outside that the back of the boot starts to lean to one side and does not sit straight above the heel.

Scheherazade: the female narrator of *The Arabian Nights,* who during one thousand and one adventurous nights saved her life by entertaining her husband, the king, with stories.

schooner: a fast sailing ship with at least two masts and with sails set lengthwise.

senhor: (Portuguese) a title of courtesy equivalent to *Mr.* or *sir.*

senhorita: (Portuguese) a title of address equivalent to *miss*; used alone or with the name of a girl or unmarried woman.

Sennar: a state in Sudan; a town on the Blue Nile and the capital of the state of Sennar.

Shanghai: city of eastern China at the mouth of the Yangtze River, and the largest city in the country. Shanghai was opened to foreign trade by treaty in 1842 and quickly prospered. France, Great Britain and the United States all held large concessions (rights to use land granted by a government) in the city until the early twentieth century.

singlet: a sleeveless undershirt.

Solomons: Solomon Islands; a group of islands northeast of Australia. They form a double chain of six large islands, about twenty medium-sized ones and numerous smaller islets and reefs.

Soroti: the main commercial and administrative center of the Soroti District in eastern Uganda, a country in East Africa bordered on the east by Kenya and the north by Sudan.

strike: in mining and geology, the linear course or direction of a layer of rock or vein. The strike of a vein is at right angles to the direction of the dip (the downward slope of the layer of rock or vein).

stringers: narrow veins or irregular threads of minerals.

Sudan Railway: railway system in Sudan, linking most of the major towns and cities. Sudan is bordered by Egypt to the north, the Red Sea to the northeast, Ethiopia to the east and Kenya and Uganda to the southwest. The first line was built in the 1870s and was a commercial undertaking. It was extended in the mid-1880s and again in the mid-1890s to support the Anglo-Egyptian military campaigns.

Taku: site of forts built in the 1500s to defend Tientsin against foreign invasion. The forts are located by the Hai River, 37 miles (60 km) southeast of Tientsin.

Tanganyika: a former country of east-central Africa. A British territory after 1920, it became independent in 1961 and joined with Zanzibar to form Tanzania in 1964.

Timor: an island at the south end of a cluster of islands located between mainland southeastern Asia and Australia. The island has been politically divided in two parts for centuries: West Timor, which was known as Dutch Timor from the 1800s until 1949 when it became Indonesian Timor; and East Timor, which was known as Portuguese Timor from 1596 until 1975.

Timor Laut: a group of about thirty islands in the Maluku (Spice Islands) province of Indonesia.

trail, at: trail arms; to hold a rifle in the right hand at an oblique angle, with the muzzle forward and the butt a few inches off the ground.

transit: a surveying instrument surmounted by a telescope that can be rotated completely around its horizontal axis, used for measuring vertical and horizontal angles.

Tsavo: a region of Kenya located at the crossing of the Uganda Railway over the Tsavo River. It is the largest national park in Kenya and one of the largest in the world. Because of its size the park was split into two, Tsavo West and Tsavo East, for easy administration. Tsavo achieved fame in *The Man-eaters of Tsavo*, a book about lions who attacked workers building the railroad bridge.

Uganda Railway: a historical railway system linking the interiors of Uganda and Kenya to the Indian Ocean at Mombasa in Kenya. The line started at the port city of Mombasa in 1896 and reached Kisuma in 1901 on the eastern shore of Lake Victoria. Despite being called "the Lunatic Line" by its detractors, the railway was a huge logistical achievement and became strategically and economically vital for both Uganda and Kenya.

weather eye: alertness and watchfulness, especially an alertness to change.

wire gold: gold ore that looks like its description: fine, short pieces of wire, or a tangled wirelike mass. It is found mostly in pockets or veins.

witch doctor: a person who is believed to heal through magical powers.

Yank: Yankee; term used to refer to Americans in general.

ye: you.

L. Ron Hubbard
in the Golden Age
of Pulp Fiction

*In writing an adventure story
a writer has to know that he is adventuring
for a lot of people who cannot.
The writer has to take them here and there
about the globe and show them
excitement and love and realism.
As long as that writer is living the part of an
adventurer when he is hammering
the keys, he is succeeding with his story.*

*Adventuring is a state of mind.
If you adventure through life, you have a
good chance to be a success on paper.*

*Adventure doesn't mean globe-trotting,
exactly, and it doesn't mean great deeds.
Adventuring is like art.
You have to live it to make it real.*

— L. RON HUBBARD

L. Ron Hubbard
and American
Pulp Fiction

B ORN March 13, 1911, L. Ron Hubbard lived a life at least as expansive as the stories with which he enthralled a hundred million readers through a fifty-year career.

Originally hailing from Tilden, Nebraska, he spent his formative years in a classically rugged Montana, replete with the cowpunchers, lawmen and desperadoes who would later people his Wild West adventures. And lest anyone imagine those adventures were drawn from vicarious experience, he was not only breaking broncs at a tender age, he was also among the few whites ever admitted into Blackfoot society as a bona fide blood brother. While if only to round out an otherwise rough and tumble youth, his mother was that rarity of her time—a thoroughly educated woman—who introduced her son to the classics of Occidental literature even before his seventh birthday.

But as any dedicated L. Ron Hubbard reader will attest, his world extended far beyond Montana. In point of fact, and as the son of a United States naval officer, by the age of eighteen he had traveled over a quarter of a million miles. Included therein were three Pacific crossings to a then still mysterious Asia, where he ran with the likes of Her British Majesty's agent-in-place

for North China, and the last in the line of Royal Magicians from the court of Kublai Khan. For the record, L. Ron Hubbard was also among the first Westerners to gain admittance to forbidden Tibetan monasteries below Manchuria, and his photographs of China's Great Wall long graced American geography texts.

L. Ron Hubbard, left, at Congressional Airport, Washington, DC, 1931, with members of George Washington University flying club.

Upon his return to the United States and a hasty completion of his interrupted high school education, the young Ron Hubbard entered George Washington University. There, as fans of his aerial adventures may have heard, he earned his wings as a pioneering barnstormer at the dawn of American aviation. He also earned a place in free-flight record books for the longest sustained flight above Chicago. Moreover, as a roving reporter for *Sportsman Pilot* (featuring his first professionally penned articles), he further helped inspire a generation of pilots who would take America to world airpower.

Immediately beyond his sophomore year, Ron embarked on the first of his famed ethnological expeditions, initially to then untrammeled Caribbean shores (descriptions of which would later fill a whole series of West Indies mystery-thrillers). That the Puerto Rican interior would also figure into the future of Ron Hubbard stories was likewise no accident. For in addition to cultural studies of the island, a 1932–33

LRH expedition is rightly remembered as conducting the first complete mineralogical survey of a Puerto Rico under United States jurisdiction.

There was many another adventure along this vein: As a lifetime member of the famed Explorers Club, L. Ron Hubbard charted North Pacific waters with the first shipboard radio direction finder, and so pioneered a long-range navigation system universally employed until the late twentieth century. While not to put too fine an edge on it, he also held a rare Master Mariner's license to pilot any vessel, of any tonnage in any ocean.

Yet lest we stray too far afield, there is an LRH note at this juncture in his saga, and it reads in part:

"I started out writing for the pulps, writing the best I knew, writing for every mag on the stands, slanting as well as I could."

To which one might add: His earliest submissions date from the

Capt. L. Ron Hubbard in Ketchikan, Alaska, 1940, on his Alaskan Radio Experimental Expedition, the first of three voyages conducted under the Explorers Club flag.

summer of 1934, and included tales drawn from true-to-life Asian adventures, with characters roughly modeled on British/American intelligence operatives he had known in Shanghai. His early Westerns were similarly peppered with details drawn from personal experience. Although therein lay a first hard lesson from the often cruel world of the pulps. His first Westerns were soundly rejected as lacking the authenticity of a Max Brand yarn (a particularly frustrating comment given L. Ron Hubbard's Westerns came straight from his Montana homeland, while Max Brand was a mediocre New York poet named Frederick Schiller Faust, who turned out implausible six-shooter tales from the terrace of an Italian villa).

Nevertheless, and needless to say, L. Ron Hubbard persevered and soon earned a reputation as among the most publishable names in pulp fiction, with a ninety percent placement rate of first-draft manuscripts. He was also among the most prolific, averaging between seventy and a hundred thousand words a month. Hence the rumors that L. Ron Hubbard had redesigned a typewriter for faster keyboard action and pounded out manuscripts on a continuous roll of butcher paper to save the precious seconds it took to insert a single sheet of paper into manual typewriters of the day.

That all L. Ron Hubbard stories did not run beneath said byline is yet another aspect of pulp fiction lore. That is, as publishers periodically rejected manuscripts from top-drawer authors if only to avoid paying top dollar, L. Ron Hubbard and company just as frequently replied with submissions under various pseudonyms. In Ron's case, the

A MAN OF MANY NAMES

*Between 1934 and 1950,
L. Ron Hubbard authored more than
fifteen million words of fiction in more
than two hundred classic publications.
To supply his fans and editors with
stories across an array of genres and
pulp titles, he adopted fifteen pseudonyms
in addition to his already renowned
L. Ron Hubbard byline.*

*Winchester Remington Colt
Lt. Jonathan Daly
Capt. Charles Gordon
Capt. L. Ron Hubbard
Bernard Hubbel
Michael Keith
Rene Lafayette
Legionnaire 148
Legionnaire 14830
Ken Martin
Scott Morgan
Lt. Scott Morgan
Kurt von Rachen
Barry Randolph
Capt. Humbert Reynolds*

list included: Rene Lafayette, Captain Charles Gordon, Lt. Scott Morgan and the notorious Kurt von Rachen—supposedly on the lam for a murder rap, while hammering out two-fisted prose in Argentina. The point: While L. Ron Hubbard as Ken Martin spun stories of Southeast Asian intrigue, LRH as Barry Randolph authored tales of

L. Ron Hubbard, circa 1930, at the outset of a literary career that would finally span half a century.

romance on the Western range—which, stretching between a dozen genres is how he came to stand among the two hundred elite authors providing close to a million tales through the glory days of American Pulp Fiction.

In evidence of exactly that, by 1936 L. Ron Hubbard was literally leading pulp fiction's elite as president of New York's American Fiction Guild. Members included a veritable pulp hall of fame: Lester "Doc Savage" Dent, Walter "The Shadow" Gibson, and the legendary Dashiell Hammett—to cite but a few.

Also in evidence of just where L. Ron Hubbard stood within his first two years on the American pulp circuit: By the spring of 1937, he was ensconced in Hollywood, adopting a Caribbean thriller for Columbia Pictures, remembered today as *The Secret of Treasure Island*. Comprising fifteen thirty-minute episodes, the L. Ron Hubbard screenplay led to the most profitable matinée serial in Hollywood history. In accord with Hollywood culture, he was thereafter continually called upon

The 1937 Secret of Treasure Island, *a fifteen-episode serial adapted for the screen by L. Ron Hubbard from his novel,* Murder at Pirate Castle.

to rewrite/doctor scripts—most famously for long-time friend and fellow adventurer Clark Gable.

In the interim—and herein lies another distinctive chapter of the L. Ron Hubbard story—he continually worked to open Pulp Kingdom gates to up-and-coming authors. Or, for that matter, anyone who wished to write. It was a fairly unconventional stance, as markets were already thin and competition razor sharp. But the fact remains, it was an L. Ron Hubbard hallmark that he vehemently lobbied on behalf of young authors—regularly supplying instructional articles to trade journals, guest-lecturing to short story classes at George Washington University and Harvard, and even founding his own creative writing competition. It was established in 1940, dubbed the Golden Pen, and guaranteed winners both New York representation and publication in *Argosy*.

But it was John W. Campbell Jr.'s *Astounding Science Fiction* that finally proved the most memorable LRH vehicle. While every fan of L. Ron Hubbard's galactic epics undoubtedly knows the story, it nonetheless bears repeating: By late 1938, the pulp publishing magnate of Street & Smith was determined to revamp *Astounding Science Fiction* for broader readership. In particular, senior editorial director F. Orlin Tremaine called for stories with a stronger *human element*. When acting editor John W. Campbell balked, preferring his spaceship-driven

112

tales, Tremaine enlisted Hubbard. Hubbard, in turn, replied with the genre's first truly *character-driven* works, wherein heroes are pitted not against bug-eyed monsters but the mystery and majesty of deep space itself—and thus was launched the Golden Age of Science Fiction.

The names alone are enough to quicken the pulse of any science fiction aficionado, including LRH friend and protégé, Robert Heinlein, Isaac Asimov, A. E. van Vogt and Ray Bradbury. Moreover, when coupled with LRH stories of fantasy, we further come to what's rightly been described as the foundation of every modern tale of horror: L. Ron Hubbard's immortal *Fear.* It was rightly proclaimed by Stephen King as one of the very few works to genuinely warrant that overworked term "classic"—as in: *"This is a classic tale of creeping, surreal menace and horror. . . . This is one of the really, really good ones."*

L. Ron Hubbard, 1948, among fellow science fiction luminaries at the World Science Fiction Convention in Toronto.

To accommodate the greater body of L. Ron Hubbard fantasies, Street & Smith inaugurated *Unknown*—a classic pulp if there ever was one, and wherein readers were soon thrilling to the likes of *Typewriter in the Sky* and *Slaves of Sleep* of which Frederik Pohl would declare: *"There are bits and pieces from Ron's work that became part of the language in ways that very few other writers managed."*

And, indeed, at J. W. Campbell Jr.'s insistence, Ron was regularly drawing on themes from the Arabian Nights and so introducing readers to a world of genies, jinn, Aladdin and Sinbad—all of which, of course, continue to float through cultural mythology to this day.

At least as influential in terms of post-apocalypse stories was L. Ron Hubbard's 1940 *Final Blackout*. Generally acclaimed as the finest anti-war novel of the decade and among the ten best works of the genre ever authored—here, too, was a tale that would live on in ways few other writers imagined.

Portland, Oregon, 1943; L. Ron Hubbard, captain of the US Navy subchaser PC 815.

Hence, the later Robert Heinlein verdict: "Final Blackout *is as perfect a piece of science fiction as has ever been written.*"

Like many another who both lived and wrote American pulp adventure, the war proved a tragic end to Ron's sojourn in the pulps. He served with distinction in four theaters and was highly decorated for commanding corvettes in the North Pacific. He was also grievously wounded in combat, lost many a close friend and colleague and thus resolved to say farewell to pulp fiction and devote himself to what it had supported these many years—namely, his serious research.

But in no way was the LRH literary saga at an end, for as he wrote some thirty years later, in 1980:

"Recently there came a period when I had little to do. This was novel in a life so crammed with busy years, and I decided to amuse myself by writing a novel that was pure *science fiction."*

That work was *Battlefield Earth: A Saga of the Year 3000*. It was an immediate *New York Times* bestseller and, in fact, the first international science fiction blockbuster in decades. It was not, however, L. Ron Hubbard's magnum opus, as that distinction is generally reserved for his next and final work: The 1.2 million word *Mission Earth*.

> **Final Blackout**
> *is as perfect a piece of science fiction as has ever been written.*
>
> —Robert Heinlein

How he managed those 1.2 million words in just over twelve months is yet another piece of the L. Ron Hubbard legend. But the fact remains, he did indeed author a ten-volume *dekalogy* that lives in publishing history for the fact that each and every volume of the series was also a *New York Times* bestseller.

Moreover, as subsequent generations discovered L. Ron Hubbard through republished works and novelizations of his screenplays, the mere fact of his name on a cover signaled an international bestseller. . . . Until, to date, sales of his works exceed hundreds of millions, and he otherwise remains among the most enduring and widely read authors in literary history. Although as a final word on the tales of L. Ron Hubbard, perhaps it's enough to simply reiterate what editors told readers in the glory days of American Pulp Fiction:

He writes the way he does, brothers, because he's been there, seen it and done it!

THE STORIES FROM THE GOLDEN AGE

Your ticket to adventure starts here with the Stories from
the Golden Age collection by master storyteller L. Ron Hubbard.
These gripping tales are set in a kaleidoscope of exotic locales and brim
with fascinating characters, including some of the
most vile villains, dangerous dames and brazen heroes
you'll ever get to meet.

The entire collection of over one hundred and fifty stories is being
released in a series of eighty books and audiobooks.
For an up-to-date listing of available titles,
go to www.goldenagestories.com.

AIR ADVENTURE

FAR-FLUNG ADVENTURE

SEA ADVENTURE

TALES FROM THE ORIENT

MYSTERY

119

FANTASY

SCIENCE FICTION

WESTERN